What about Jayne?

C Fleming

1

Maxine Carver would say that she led a happy life. Teaching aerobics to a bunch of bored housewives four times a week at the over-priced day spa before going back to her whitewashed ivy-strewn cottage in the village contented her. Husband Grant was perfect. He spent a large portion of the week living away on business, which gave her ample 'me time', yet he earned enough to pay for their comfortable lifestyle.

On this particular Friday, she left Brook Hall with the usual spring in her step. As an employee, she was permitted to use the facilities, so she spent ages in the posh showers, washing the beads of sweat from her fox-coloured hair. She carefully applied straighteners so that it flowed down to her shoulders in a healthy rich shimmer. She shoved her damp t-shirt and leggings ruthlessly inside her gym bag and wrapped her talcum-powdered body in low cut jeans and a skimpy orange wrap-around cardigan that allowed her to show off a belly button ring that glistened with pride on her flat stomach. Gucci shades completed the outfit, as Maxine strode off towards her Mini Cooper in the car park.

"Will I see you tomorrow for the ab blast class?" Mrs Eaton called after her across the lobby. She had also shed her soggy gym clothes in favour of the standard spa-issue white towelling robe. No doubt she would be heading into the restaurant next and replacing all the calories she had just burned in Maxine's class before sleeping off the exertion on a lounger around the glistening pool.

"No, not tomorrow," Maxine replied. "It's Saturday. I don't work weekends."

She checked herself in the mirror behind Mrs Eaton's back – a regular habit that Grant found highly irritating. It frustrated her to note that the shade of lipstick wasn't quite right with the cardigan.

"Are you doing anything nice?"

Maxine hated that question. What was nice to her – taking a deep bath and reading the latest copy of Cosmopolitan magazine, having a manicure, writing a long letter to Grant on lavender scented notepaper – was not very interesting to others.

"Not really. I have a lot of housework to catch up on," she lied. The cleaner would have already been in today, tidying the stacks of magazines from the floor, putting CDs back in cases and trying to squeeze stray items of clothing back into Maxine's overflowing wardrobe. Those tasks took longer than the washing-up, dusting and vacuuming put together.

"Well, have a lovely weekend. Maybe I'll see you next Friday?" Maxine waved goodbye to Mrs Eaton and hurried out to the car.

She wasn't a fast driver, but today she nudged the edges of the speed limits in her impatience to get home and see how Tony was getting on. He'd arrived at her cottage promptly that morning as arranged, and she'd left him with the task in hand whilst she popped out to do her shift. She hoped he'd be finished by now, but three hours to complete the job was a tall order, she presumed.

The countryside flashed by outside her windows, the hedgerows looking damp and drab in the weak February sunlight. The weather was warmer than of late, and Maxine hoped that the promise of spring was around the corner. She loved it when the cherry blossom burst to life, adorning the churchyard with the colour of romance. It wouldn't be long before the daffodils poked their tenacious heads out of the earth in defiance of the long winter months and spread their yellow joy in the most unlikely of places.

She would repaint the picket fence in the spring, she decided, as she walked up the front garden path. It was showing signs of neglect and, as the first thing people saw as they arrived at the cottage, it needed to be neat and bright white to match the whitewash of the house.

Excitedly, she entered the hallway and trotted up the stairs to the landing. Tony was squatting over his toolbox, packing the last of the instruments away.

"Ah," he beamed. "I'm just about finished. Let me give you a demonstration."

Maxine looked up to the loft hatch, and back to Tony with a big smile on her face. Grant would be so pleased with what she'd done. Her valentine's gift to him. Tony brandished a pole with a hook on the end.

"You grab the latch like so, and pull the door ajar." He unhooked the pole and joined it to the metal beast that was poking from the gloom. "Then you can slide the ladder half way. Simply unclamp the side like so..." Maxine watched the demonstration carefully. "And the rest slides down easily. Voila!"

He gave the steps a shove to demonstrate how safe and reliable they would be, then reversed the process and packed the folding ladder back into its lair, before inviting Maxine to try for herself. She took the pole, and copied his actions from a few moments ago, pleased with the ease in which

2

the mechanics allowed the sturdy ladder to uncurl from the hatch and invite her to enter the loft.

They should have done this years ago, she reflected. They'd lived in the cottage for fifteen years and, despite a previous owner boarding the loft, it was too much hassle to fetch ladders from the garage to get into it. This meant that everything from Christmas decorations, boxes of games, worn-out shoes, "useful" cardboard boxes and old photograph albums got dumped in the spare bedroom instead.

Her parents move to Spain a year ago added to the mess. They made the decision to retire to the sunshine of the Costa del Sol and put their pub on the market. Both Maxine and her sister, Trudy, were ordered to come and collect any remaining possessions. Her childhood now lay in faded cardboard boxes in the cottage spare room waiting to be tended to.

Grant arrived home from London just after 7pm, a little later than usual due to the volume of traffic clogging up the M1. It seemed to be getting worse each week, with thousands of workers, just like Grant, fleeing the city for the weekend. It didn't put him in the best of moods, but once Maxine had calmed him down with a cup of tea and the promise of a delicious lamb stew, he finally relaxed into his favourite armchair and sighed, letting the stresses of London life escape his body.

Maxine regarded him from her temporary perch on the arm of the sofa. She itched to show him what she'd done, but he detested his relaxation being interrupted. His tea was still steaming and he hadn't yet changed from his London uniform to his home attire. He'd got as far as loosening his tie and kicking off his shiny leather shoes but, until he'd had time to change into his jeans and t-shirt, Maxine knew not to bother him.

"I've got something to show you," she grinned, when he was back into village mode.

He rolled his eyes, but followed her up the stairs and watched while she demonstrated the ladder.

"Ta-dah!" she exclaimed, indicating the loft access like a stewardess pointing out the nearest emergency exit. "What do you think? I can now clear all the stuff from the spare room."

"Great," he replied, without the enthusiasm she was hoping for. He checked the ladder, inspecting the craftsmanship as though not trusting Maxine to have got a qualified tradesman to carry out the work. It was a habit he carried over from his life as a property developer, where he constantly double-checked that contractors weren't cutting corners or working to a substandard specification. He gave a nod, which Maxine took as approval and, as the ladder was down, she calculated that she had thirty minutes to make a start before the lamb would be ready.

Grant made no offer to help, and disappeared back downstairs to put the TV on. She didn't need his help anyway, she figured, picking through the first box. Shoes. So many shoes. She ought to have a cull, she thought guiltily, but you never know when certain shoes will be useful. She heaved the box up into the loft space, marvelling at the extra room she would now have. She gazed around the expanse and figured that she could get some racking installed to display the shoes. Yes, that would make it easy to see exactly what she had.

Clambering back down the ladder, her eyes fell on the stack of photo albums. Nostalgically, she nestled into the floor and slid the first album onto her lap. In her childhood writing, a red felt tip pen had been used to scrawl "Clover Bay 1981" on the cover. Where did those thirty years go, she wondered. She opened up to the first page. There was the first ever photo that she had taken with the Brownie camera her parents bought her on her tenth birthday. It showed her twin sister, Trudy, standing under a tree in the park, with a toothy grin and a self-conscious stance. The photo was a little blurred as she must have shaken the camera as she pressed the shutter. The next one, still blurry, was taken at Christmas, with all the customers in her parents' pub, enjoying drinks before closing time. The crowd of regulars from "five-pints Freddy" to "Benny Bacardi" were gathered in a euphoric huddle, raising their glasses to the camera. She could remember begging her mum to allow her to enter the bar to take the picture. Normally out of bounds, her mum relented on this occasion as it was Christmas, after all.

As Maxine turned each page, she was drawn further into 1981. Pictures of long deceased distant family members, random snaps of cars, pets, birthday parties, school friends and trips away made for a nostalgic wander down memory lane. She turned the final page and a larger photograph tumbled loose from its resting place against the back cover. A printed photograph in black and white that her mum had purchased from the newspaper offices after it had appeared in the Clover Bay Echo. Maxine smiled fondly as she gazed at the group gathered like a happy family in front of Big Ben.

She ran her index finger over the faces one by one. On the left was her non-identical twin, Trudy, that same toothy grin, and strands of her hair worked loose from her pigtails. Her arm was around Fiona Farr, whose smile was always guarded. Fiona's Mediterranean complexion made her seem more exotic than the others, her dark eyes glowering at the camera as though she were challenging the lens in some way. In the centre was Jayne. Gosh, she hadn't given Jayne a thought in years. She was dominant in the way that she got to hold the trophy in the picture, displaying it to the camera with the confident, self-assured smile of a beauty queen. What was her surname? Maxine racked her brains, and flipped the photo over to read her own handwritten scrawl from thirty years ago. "Trudy, Fiona Farr, Jayne Gray and Leon Batty - with Miss Earle. 28th June 1981."

She flipped the picture back to the smiling faces. On Leon's cheeks, someone had splurged a blob of red felt tip pen, reflecting his tendency to blush on every occasion. "Blusher Batty" was how kids mocked him, not unfairly. He would turn crimson every time a teacher asked him a question, or anybody spoke directly to him. Bless him. His little baby face grinned at the camera, with Miss Earle crouched at the end with her hand placed casually on Leon's shoulder.

In four months from now, the picture would be thirty years old, Maxine calculated. Apart from Trudy, she hadn't seen this gang since leaving junior school. Everyone would have turned forty by now, especially Miss Earle, who would be in her mid-fifties. She looked back at the faces. Would Fiona still look that mysterious? Was Leon still baby-faced? And what about Jayne? Wherever did she go after that summer of 1981?

"Isn't the casserole ready yet?" Grant asked, poking his head into the doorway, snapping Maxine back to the present.

"Er, yes, I'll dish up," she replied obediently, rising to her feet. She closed the photo album but left the loose picture out, and placed it on the dressing table. A plan was forming in her head. It was time to get the gang back together.

2

Susie Earle looked out over the school playing field where the rain swept determinedly at forty-five degrees. Plans for rounders would have to be scrapped, but it meant she could divert attention to the quiz instead. Choosing the team would be tricky. There were some competitive individuals in this year group and it could all end in jealousy and tears.

On hearing her name, Susie rose from her plastic seat, stationed at the side of the makeshift stage and approached the centre, where Mr Martin nodded at her and stepped aside.

"Thank you, Mr Martin. That's right, we have some exciting news. Hands up if you watch Mastermind on telly?"

She scanned the faces of the children sat cross-legged on the polished gym floor. They all stared up at her eagerly, and several hands shot up. Jayne Gray's hand was first, like a rocket. It was a given that she watched Mastermind. She probably lapped up University Challenge too, Susie reflected. Leon Batty raised a hesitant hand, and blushed when Miss Earle's eyes skimmed over him. None of the council estate kids put up their hands, but there was a decent proportion of the fourth years who at least knew what Mastermind was.

"No, you don't," Trudy hissed at her twin sister as Maxine thrust her hand up.

"I do, too," Maxine retorted.

"Liar."

"OK, you can put your hands down, and it's great to see so many quiz fans out there," Miss Earle continued. "The reason I asked that question is because there is a national quiz championship for primary schools every year. Schools from all over the country compete to win a big trophy and I have some exciting news. For the first time, Mr Martin has agreed that Clover Bay Primary School can put a team together to take part!"

There was a small gasp of anticipation, but it was more to do with Miss Earle's enthusiastic delivery than the realities of a national quiz. "So, we need just four people to form the quiz team, and to help us choose who will be representing the school, your form teachers will be handing out quiz sheets during this morning's lessons. You don't have to have a go if you don't want to. It's completely up to you. If you do choose to complete a quiz, you MUST do it by yourself and not ask anybody else the answers. OK?"

As the children traipsed out of the hall twenty minutes later, Miss Earle guessed that the enthusiastic quiz contestants would be the same pupils that always wanted to be involved in school activities. It was always the same dozen children who signed up to take part in the Nativity plays, played on the school sports teams, and sang carols to patients in the local hospital. They would be the same ones taking harvest festival produce to the nursing home up the road next week. Only this time, enthusiasm wasn't going to be enough. She needed the brightest, sharpest brains, combined with a calm demeanour to cope with the pressure of live quizzing. Whilst there were several pupils whose competitive streak shone through, Miss Earle herself was the biggest culprit. Just because this was a run-of-the-mill school in a sleepy seaside backwater, there was no reason her team couldn't stomp all over those posh, privately educated kids. Oh yes, she was going to bring the trophy home for Clover Bay Primary.

"I have to be on this team," Jayne declared to the twins as they sat in the classroom later that morning. They had been set a task of colouring in a picture of Sir Francis Drake, having heard about his exploits on the high seas, but Jayne's mind was on the sheet that had just been presented to her. Fifty quiz questions typed in neat rows with a gap for the answer.

Next to her, Maxine glanced down at the first few questions on the sheet and felt her heart sink. She didn't know the answers to any of these. She glanced over the table at Trudy, who had wrapped a protective arm around her sheet to shield the answers from prying eyes and was leaning low over the table so that her thick hair provided a curtain to fill the gap.

Jayne folded her quiz sheet in half and placed it to one side. "I'll do mine at home tonight," she explained.

"What about you, Darren?" Maxine asked the skinny, quiet kid opposite her. "Are you going to do the quiz?"

He peered at the questions and screwed up his nose. "Nah, I hate quizzes. They're for swots."

"Well, I thought perhaps we could do it together?"

"You heard Miss Earle. We must do it by ourselves," Darren retorted. "Otherwise, it's cheating."

Maxine sighed and folded her quiz sheet in half as Jayne had done. She would take it home too and try to tease the answers out of anyone she could. She started with Pete, the chef that worked in her parents' pub. The term 'chef' was probably an exaggeration. He took battered chicken or scampi pieces from large catering packs and spread them on a baking tray and oven cooked them until golden, along with chips that bubbled in the deep fat fryer. It was all served in a basket with a tiny garnish of parsley, which the majority of customers removed and abandoned on the side of their plate. Pete had been a loyal employee for as long as Maxine could remember, serving up meals five nights a week from the Five Bells' steamed-up kitchen.

"Are you going to help me?" he asked Maxine, as she hovered in the kitchen doorway that evening. "I could use a hand chopping up some tomatoes for the prawn cocktail garnish."

Maxine nodded and clambered onto the stool at the end of the table where she wouldn't get in the way. Pete pushed a chopping board in her direction as he did on the many occasions that Maxine offered to help out. With Trudy tucked away with her nose in a book and her parents serving at the bar, Maxine often sought Pete's company in the evenings, and her parents didn't object as long as she wasn't given the sharpest knives or allowed near the cavernous oven.

She'd brought the quiz sheet to the kitchen and glanced furtively at the questions in her lap.

"So," she began, as she carefully sliced the first tomato into chunky quarters. "Why do some people classify tomatoes as a fruit?"

Pete glanced up, suspicious. What was Maxine doing using big words like 'classify'?

"I think it's something to do with having seeds," he replied.

"Do you know which motorway goes from Taunton to Exeter?"

Pete paused from where he was cutting a slice of lemon meringue pie and glanced up at her.

"It's to settle an argument at school," she clarified, sensing that he was going to ask why she wanted to know. She didn't want to admit to the cheating on the quiz questions in case Trudy were to find out.

Tony laughed and shrugged. "I can't help you there. I don't drive, do I? I would go by train if I wanted to do that journey."

Disheartened, Maxine glanced at the next question, which concerned where the father was taken in The Railway Children. Trudy would know this one, of course. She was bound to have consumed the book.

"Have you read The Railway Children?" she asked Pete.

"What's that, a book?" he asked with a chuckle. "I can't remember the last time I read any books."

"What, not even at school?"

He stopped, poised with the jug of cream in his hand and thought. School was a long time ago, and there weren't a lot of books going spare in the war years. Reading was never something he felt compelled to do later in life. He was more a doer, rather than sitting around with his nose in a book. He like to make stuff, creating things with his hands, that was more his style. He shook his head.

Maxine sighed and shoved the quiz sheet back into her pocket. This was clearly harder than she first envisioned. She was going to have to be sneaky to become part of the quiz team.

3

Lennox Street, where Trudy had lived since 1988, stretched for nearly half a mile, with over three hundred terraced houses standing tall and proud on both sides of the cramped road. Parking was a nightmare, of course, with no households having the luxury of a driveway, so Maxine cursed under her breath as she hunted for that elusive space. She managed to find a gap just a few hundred metres from Trudy's front door, so that wasn't too bad, she reasoned, as she reverse-parked in and killed the engine. The three-hour drive exhausted her and she was glad that she wouldn't have to travel back up to the Midlands for a couple of days.

She clambered out and retrieved her compact suitcase from the boot, along with a carrier bag containing her offering to the host: a chocolate cake and a bottle of wine. She wasn't sure if it was good wine - Grant was in charge of stocking the wine rack at home, and she'd just grabbed one with a pretty label with some flowers on. Trudy and Jason would never be able to tell the difference any more than she could.

She breathed in deeply, the sea air evident even this far back from the beach. A couple of fat seagulls swooped overhead with a chortling squawk that sounded as though they were mocking her. She didn't miss the seagulls, but generally the return to her hometown filled her with nostalgia.

Trudy opened the door with a flurry of apologies about how she'd only just got back from work, later than she'd planned, so Maxine was to excuse the mess as she hadn't had time to put the Hoover around. The sisters hugged and Maxine followed Trudy through the narrow hallway into the kitchen at the rear. Plastic carrier bags were strewn across the counter tops, half unpacked.

"Grab a seat. Just let me put away the frozen stuff and then I'll get the kettle on," Trudy explained as she rifled into the bags to seek out the items that needed her urgent attention. "Good journey?"

"Not bad," replied Maxine, omitting the detail of the tortuous roadworks on the M5 around Birmingham that brought traffic to a crawl for around ten miles, and the tedious approach to Clover Bay where junction after junction teased her with a red traffic light. Still, she had set off early enough to get to Trudy's house before the winter darkness descended.

"I had plans to make a lasagne from scratch, but time just got away from me," Trudy apologised, "so I resorted to buying one. It'll probably taste a lot more palatable, to be honest."

Rejecting Maxine's offer of help, Trudy continued to buzz around the kitchen, packing groceries into cupboards whilst making cups of tea and listening to Maxine's small talk about what was new since they last spoke.

Trudy's husband, Jason, crashed through the back door just after five o'clock, his cheerful grin brightening up the kitchen as the last of the afternoon light faded outside. He wore beige overalls and battered trainers. His uniform was topped off with an ageing fleece jacket bearing the Clover Bay Primary School motif on the breast. Maxine found it fascinating that he worked as the caretaker in the school where he was a pupil thirty years earlier. He kept the sisters updated on staff comings and goings, school politics, and whose kids were most likely to end up in prison within a decade.

"Hi, Aunty Max." Eleven-year-old Robbie appeared from the hallway and greeted Maxine politely before opening the fridge. She was fond of the boys. All three of Trudy's offspring had grown up with courteous manners and self-belief. The eldest, Ben, had been born when Trudy was just seventeen. Not that he'd been a mistake. Both Trudy and Jason left school at sixteen and, to the horror of their parents, rejected sixth form and got engaged. With the financial help of Jason's grandparents, they quickly got married and put a deposit down on the house on Lennox Street, losing no time in starting their family. The house was a dilapidated mess when they bought it, which meant it was affordable, of course. With Jason's natural skills at DIY, he embraced the project, updating the rooms one by one, modernising the property and turning it into both a home and a valuable asset.

Trudy fell pregnant quickly and Ben came along in 1989. How the years had flown; he was now a homeowner himself, having bought a project "in need of modernisation" whilst working long hours as a plumber.

James was born three years later, and was still finding his true vocation in life. Having gained some decent A-level grades, he took off to the south of France on a gap year and ended up working the deckhand life on yachts whose insurance premiums alone were greater than the cost of the Lennox Street house. The gap year had extended to two years, and showed no signs of ending any time soon.

This left Robbie as the youngest of the clan. Although Trudy would never admit it, Maxine swore he had been born to prevent Trudy having an empty nest so soon. There was still five years before Robbie would be going anywhere.

"Are you going running in the morning?" Robbie asked Maxine. She always brought her kit to Clover Bay and this trip was no exception. When she nodded, he asked if he could join her.

"It's a school day, young man," Trudy scolded him. "So, unless Maxine is going out really early, you won't be back in time for school. And what are you eating?"

Robbie scrutinised the treasure he'd plucked from the fridge. "A salami stick. And no, I won't spoil my appetite; I'm a growing lad."

Trudy couldn't help grinning at her son. "Don't feel obliged to have him tagging along," she advised.

"If it's not icy, I'll be going out about six, and back by seven. If you want to join me, and can keep up, you're welcome."

"You're on," Robbie nodded his acceptance of the challenge, and disappeared from the kitchen. Maxine didn't want to deter anyone from running. She was Robbie's age when she first got inspired to run long distances. She could remember it clearly. It was the first ever London marathon that whet her appetite, and it was being televised. Maxine had sat cross-legged in the lounge, watching the runners on the screen with awe. They passed so many London landmarks and, as they strode up The Mall towards the finish line, they appeared to have as much energy as they had when they started the race twenty six miles earlier. There was much fuss and jubilation as the first woman crossed the finish line. Joyce Smith was not only home-grown talent, but she was the first British woman to run a marathon in less than two and a half hours.

"Mum, do you think I could win the London marathon?" she asked, as her mother hurried through the lounge on a mission to fetch more cigarettes to fill the vending machine.

She threw a cursory glance at the TV screen. "Maybe, darling. I expect that lady was your age when she started. You just need a lot of practice."

How many thousands of miles had Maxine's feet trodden since that time, she wondered? Thirty years of running, starting with school cross country events, then the middle-distance track events, joining running clubs at university, half marathons, full marathons... she'd never got close to the time set by Joyce Smith in 1981, but could run respectable times, and showed no signs of slowing as she entered her forties.

The year 1981 was the reason for her visit now and, once the lasagne had been consumed, the wine drunk and the washing-up completed, Maxine cut to the chase.

They remained at the kitchen table, where Jason made coffee and Robbie retreated to his room to finish his homework.

"He's probably having a sneaky game on his PlayStation," Trudy moaned, but made no move to check up on him.

Maxine rifled into her handbag and pulled out the photo that she had unearthed the week before.

"So, I brought this," she announced. Trudy took it from her and a grin started to spread across her face.

"Oh my God, I remember this. The school quiz championship. Jason, look."

Her husband turned from the counter top and took the print from her. He chuckled.

"You don't look a day older," he joked. "And just look at Blusher Batty! He was so puny back then. He's filled out now though, he still lives up at that farm at Wick Hill. Apparently he's turned it into a goldmine."

He handed the photo back to Trudy and turned back to his coffee-making duty.

"Fiona Farr. I wonder what happened to her. And what was her name?"

Trudy pointed to the blonde girl holding the trophy.

"Jayne Gray."

"Oh, that's right. She had horses, didn't she? Her mum called trousers 'pants', which we thought was hilarious."

They sat in silence for a few moments, Trudy processing the memory.

"That photo was taken thirty years ago in June. So, I had this mad idea that we could perhaps track everyone down, have a trip to London and recreate the photograph?"

Trudy looked at her sister and raised her eyebrows. "Do you think we'll be able to find them? And even if we do, will they want to come? Some people get really funny about reunions."

"Well, it's easy enough to find Blusher," Jason chipped in, placing the coffee on the table between them and taking his seat. "He's only a few miles away. But Jayne vanished after that summer, and I haven't seen Fiona since leaving school."

"What about Miss Earle?" Maxine asked as casually as she could. "That would be so cool if we could get her into the photo too."

"She left Clover Bay Primary back in the eighties," Jason confirmed, "but I reckon the Head could track her down if you're serious. I can ask if you like."

"I doubt that she'd want to come, but it's worth asking," Maxine replied. She took the photograph back from her sister and took one last look at Miss Earle's cheeky grin before stowing the image back into her handbag. Miss Earle had influenced the path of her life more than anyone knew and it would be equally terrifying and exhilarating to come back together again after all these years.

4

Susie Earle sank into the squishy chair in the staff room and sighed heavily. The first term of the year was always the busiest, going straight from harvest festival to planning for the Christmas Nativity, whilst squeezing in the festive fundraising fayre and the quiz championships on top. To be fair, she had brought the latter stress on herself. It had been her idea; she'd instigated their entry just because her ex had taken up a job at London's prestigious Westminster School, whose team had taken the crown earlier this year. For Susie, this wasn't about developing the children: this was about revenge. What a way to wipe the smug smile off his face when the lowly quizzers of Clover Bay Primary snatched the title from their privileged public school mitts.

Who was she kidding? There was a long way to go in this David and Goliath battle. First, there would be local and regional rounds to conquer before she could even begin to contemplate national domination.

She looked around the shabby room and wondered how different the facilities at the Westminster School were. They wouldn't have mismatched furniture. Why Clover Bay Primary had a blue sofa, a grey sofa and a black and white checked settee was anybody's guess. The peeling yellow paint on the walls depressed her, and the way that A4 sheets of paper had been tacked to the wall and left to fade added to the general messy atmosphere of the space.

"You look miles away." A voice jolted her back into the room. It was Adam, her closest ally at the school.

She regarded him with a smile. His shaggy mullet was dripping from the rain that still hammered the ground outside. It hadn't let up all day and the playground was dappled with puddles. Nevertheless, he'd insisted that the cycling proficiency should go ahead, an end-of-the-day soaking for the fourth years. He shivered as he shed his coat and fetched a chipped mug from the cupboard for the last cuppa of the working day.

"I've marked the quiz sheets," she replied, as though that would explain everything.

"So, who's the brain box of Clover Bay Primary?" he asked a few moments later, having drained the teapot of its last lukewarm offering. He sank into the settee opposite her and placed his mug on the wobbly coffee table. Someone had managed to damage one of its legs, leaving it unstable on the remaining three.

"Jayne Gray came top. Not much of a surprise there."

Adam nodded in agreement, remembering her in the playground just ten minutes ago, performing perfect, confident arm signalling on the pretend road layout. She had scolded Fiona Farr for getting too close and not observing a safe stopping distance. Adam despaired as Fiona retorted that her brakes didn't work, so how was she supposed to slow down?

"Then little Leon Batty came second. That's a nice surprise."

"Yes, I like Leon," agreed Adam. "He's so interested in everything. Who came third?"

"Ah. That was a three-way tie between Fiona Farr and both Waterford twins." Susie pulled a face that Adam struggled to understand. She watched his brow furrow in confusion.

"I can only have a team of four," Susie explained, "and I'm not sure that Maxine would be suitable for this. How will she react with her twin sister making it on to the team and her not quite being good enough?" She glanced down at the marked sheets and shook her head in confusion.

Adam nodded. He could see the predicament. Ten-year-old girls could be quite melodramatic when it came to life not being fair.

"Would it soften the blow if you gave Maxine a trade off? Like the lead in the Nativity?"

Susie was silent for a moment. They hadn't started to plan for the Nativity yet, and casting had to be signed off by Mr Crump so would be out of her control. Adam was onto something, though. There must be something Maxine excelled at that she could be responsible for.

"She's a fast runner," Susie stated. She remembered the school sports day back in the summer. Maxine had outrun her rivals by a long lead in the 100-metres, and brought the relay team from fourth to first on her final charge with the baton. "I could distract her with the prospect of joining the cross country team when she moves up to the comp next year. They take their cross country seriously up there." The fourth years had yet to take the eleven-plus exam, but it was a certainty that Maxine wouldn't make it to grammar school.

Adam sipped his tea and nodded. "You could. Or you could ask her to be the quiz team's lucky mascot."

In the end, Susie Earle opted for both opportunities. As the class scrambled out into the corridor at break time the following day, Miss Earle asked Maxine to stay behind for a moment.

Maxine's heart started beating faster. She couldn't think of anything she'd done that would land her in trouble, but normally when her friends had been asked to stay behind it meant they had broken some rule, or acted in a way that teachers didn't like. She didn't want Miss Earle to be cross with her.

Miss Earle sat in the seat next to Maxine and placed a newspaper in front of her. It was folded over so that it just showed the top half of the page - most of which was taken up with a photograph. It showed seven girls in a row. They looked to be a bit older than Maxine, all wearing tight shorts and t-shirts, emblazoned with numbered bibs on their front. Most had their hair scraped back into flowing pony tails and, on closer inspection, they all had muddy legs and ruddy cheeks.

"This is the crosscountry team at Clover Bay Secondary School," Miss Earle explained. "The school chooses the best runners from each year group and enters championships all across the South of England. The girls are really good, very fast, and that's why they're in the newspaper, because they win things."

Maxine was transfixed and pulled the newspaper closer to her. She could remember what it felt like to win the 100-metre race at the sports day. The cheering, the excited shouts from parents. Imagine what it would be like at a competition with bigger girls, at venues outside the confines of the Clover Bay Primary School.

"I think, when you join the big school next year, you could be chosen to represent the first years. But it means putting a lot of practice in, starting from now. Do you think you'd like to do that?"

Maxine looked at Miss Earle with wide eyes. The thought of leaving her to go to big school was terrifying, but it wasn't happening any time soon, and she could impress her teacher with her fast running times in the meantime. Oh yes, she would like to do that. She nodded.

"What I would suggest is that every time we finish games, or a netball match, when you are in your PE kit, you take the opportunity to run three laps around the school field as fast as you can. I can time you if you like and we'll see if your times get faster and faster. Yes?"

"Yes, Miss. I can also run at the weekend, along the seafront."

"What a good idea." Miss Earle smiled at her, pleased that the quiz decoy had worked. "I think you're very lucky for the school, so I've got another question to ask you. How would you like to be the lucky mascot for the school quiz team?"

Maxine's heart soared at the thought of being chosen by Miss Earle for such a prestigious role. Miss Earle thought she was special. It didn't even occur to her that she hadn't been good enough to be chosen for the quiz team itself.

5

Trudy loved it when Maxine came to stay as an array of sumptuous beauty products adorned the bathroom. She heard Maxine and Robbie leave the house whilst it was still dark, and crept out from under the covers to go and inspect what lotions and potions were on offer this time. As she suspected, Maxine had laid out an assortment of bottles along the windowsill. Vanilla soufflé body creme, said the first label. Trudy wasn't sure when to use that, so read the marketing blurb on the reverse to discover it was to be used after exfoliating. She stifled a giggle, having never exfoliated in her life. She knew they were non-identical twins, but sometimes it seemed they were from different planets.

Goddess Body Wash. Ah, now that was easier to decipher - she would wash her body with that. It was a step up from Imperial Leather. She sniffed the 'Smoothing ginger body scrub', which had a lovely aroma, but the small tube would soon be used up if Trudy squeezed that onto her sponge. Finally, the 'exceptional nutrition shampoo', came alongside a smaller bottle with the same branding. Trudy had to wade through an obscene amount of French text before concluding that this was some extra nutritional care to use after shampooing. 'Just call it conditioner!' she tutted, wondering why this would be any better than her bulky sized supermarket branded 2-in-1 that the whole family could use. It was on offer this month too.

As Trudy showered, the milky sun began to penetrate through the bathroom blind and, on the seafront, Maxine and Robbie watched as the sky turned from grey to dusky pink. They jogged in unison, Robbie's skinny legs striding confidently alongside Maxine's. The bay was a perfect running location with its wide, mile-long promenade. It was empty and quiet. There were no holiday makers here in mid-February and even if there were, none would venture out before six-thirty in the morning. Gulls soared overhead, breaking the silence with their squabbling squawks. The sea calmly rippled on the sandy shoreline, inaudible from the prom.

"I used to run along here before school too," Maxine told her nephew.

"My Mum - your Gran - wouldn't let me go further than the amusement arcade on my own, so I had to run up and down between the café and the 'muzzies' at least three times to get a decent distance in."

"I forget that you grew up here," Robbie replied. "Did Mum ever run?"

Maxine laughed. "No, running wasn't her thing. She liked reading. She always had her head in a book."

"She still does," Robbie replied with a fond smile.

They reached the amusement arcade, its shutters firmly closed for the winter. Come Easter-time, the dusty doors would be thrown open and crowds would gather amidst the hum and chaos of electronic beeping and the crash of small change. Maxine indicated that they should carry on around the back of the arcade and over the pedestrian wooden bridge that spanned the trickling stream feeding into the sea.

"Do you still like reading?" Maxine enquired, remembering how his Christmas and birthday lists resembled library catalogues.

"Oh yeah," Robbie enthused. "Mum's got me into the Zygon series. I've read the first three and there's two more to get through before the new book comes out in the summer."

"Oh, I've never heard of that," Maxine admitted. She knew she should try to read more, but never got further than thinking about it.

"They're brilliant. They're about a madcap explorer and his family who get sent off by the Government to the planet Zygon to make peace with the locals, but they get themselves into all sorts of adventures."

Maxine found her feet being drawn towards the West Cliffs, an area she hadn't been back to since childhood. A large supermarket now stood at the bottom of the hill on land where the donkey field once was.

"That's where Mum works," Robbie pointed out.

"Oh." Maxine knew that Trudy worked shifts at the local supermarket but had presumed it was the large store on the road to Tolchester. Beyond the supermarket, Maxine expected to find the single-track country lane to the West Cliffs, but instead, the road had been gauged into a wide estate road. It wound uphill as Clover Bay shrank away behind them, the open fields of the 1980s replaced with new build identical boxy houses on both sides of the road.

"Where are we going?" asked Robbie, glancing at his watch.

"Memory Lane," Maxine joked, although she was starting to wonder just how much of 1981 had been left behind. So far, the blackberry bushes were long gone, and the gravelly potholes had been replaced with smooth tarmac. Only the gradient of the hill remained consistent, and she began to puff, just as she had on her roller skates thirty years earlier. "We'll turn back once we've seen what's at the top."

As the road veered to the left, the new houses petered out, and to Maxine's relief, some greenery and paddocks reappeared. There, approaching on the horizon was the home she prayed was still there. Jayne's house.

Robbie slowed, expecting to turn around, but Maxine waved him on. "Just a bit further. Come on."

She ran alongside the low stone wall, where ivy spewed over its top and on to the entrance gates, flanked by two white stone pillars, where she halted. Robbie pulled up alongside, panting from the exertion of the hill, his breath billowing white in the frosty air. The house looked smaller than she remembered, but it remained as impressive as it was thirty years earlier. The long, low wooden sides resembled a Viking ship as they rose to two storeys at each end, and Maxine knew that on the far side, a vast pane of glass ran the length of the living space. The view over the cliff and out onto the endless open water was the breath-taking feature and added several noughts onto the price of the residence.

"I've never been up here," Robbie observed, fighting for his breath. "I think a kid in my school lives in one of the new houses. He's Scottish and talks funny. Even Miss Clarke can't understand what he says."

"Our friend lived in this house," Maxine reminisced. "With her sister and their horses. It looks as though the stables have been converted into a garage now. Their parents were from America so to us, they talked funny too." She scanned the lawn, which was manicured and similar to how she remembered it in 1981.

Robbie bounced up and down on the spot to keep warm, not particularly interested in Maxine's memories.

"Do they still live there?"

"No, they moved away before we moved up to big school."

"Where did they go?"

Maxine sighed. "That's the million-dollar question, Robbie. Where on earth did they go?" She took one last glance at the property. "Your mum and I intend to find out."

Two hours later, with Robbie at school, and Maxine showered and dressed, it was time for the sisters to venture over to Wick Hill to enlist the help of Blusher Batty into the search. Trudy offered to drive, which was a relief to Maxine who hadn't wanted to prise her car out of its tiny space. Together in the Corsa, they headed east along the seafront and out of the town past 'Tat Row', which was the unkind nickname for all the tourist shops, selling poor quality t-shirts and towels, cheap fudge and sunglasses, and plastic crap for the beach. Trudy indicated right and turned onto the quiet country lane, which thankfully hadn't been converted into an estate road. There was a brown tourist sign at the junction advertising "Wick Farm Shop and Café" a mile ahead.

"I can't believe we used to walk this distance," Trudy marvelled. "It feels a long way for junior school kids to come from the town. I wouldn't be happy for Robbie to walk up here with his mates the way we used to."

"It's a different world now, though," Maxine observed, as yet another car had to slow and pull in to let them pass. There was never as much traffic when they were kids. "Hang on. You've passed it!"

The muddy entrance to the farmhouse sailed by on the left, but Trudy carried on a little further. "I believe his parents still live in the old farmhouse, but Leon's developed this bit..." Trudy swung the car onto a gravel car park, where she had to drive to the far end to find a vacant space.

"Wow!" Maxine exclaimed. What used to be the dairy farm's old milking sheds had been converted into a large warehouse. Racks of fresh fruit and vegetables sat in colourful rows outside the front doors, whilst chalk boards advertised special events, such as a craft beer tasting, a focaccia bread making class and a sausage of the month. "Maybe we should have told him we were coming?" Maxine observed as they made their way across the gravel.

They stepped inside the shop and immediately their senses were overwhelmed with a mixture of aromas coming from the spices, laid out in "help yourself" tubs. Long shelves offered every type of condiment imaginable, whilst the butcher counter sprawled along the length of the right side.

"Look at all these different coffees!" Maxine breathed, excited by such an array of quality produce. The wine section was larger than her corner shop, wooden boxes full of straw displaying wines on their sides, like mangers from a Nativity scene. There was even a gift department, with floaty scarves, tasteful ornaments, overpriced greeting cards and framed paintings from local artists. "Jason said he'd turned this place into a goldmine."

She turned to find that Trudy was no longer by her side, but had commandeered an employee to ask where they could find Leon.

"Apparently, we can find him in the café," Trudy explained, returning to her sister's side. They shuffled through to the rear, where an archway invited them through to a large space adorned with matching wooden tables and chairs. Even though it was barely ten o'clock, the café was doing a brisk trade with customers enjoying coffee, toasted teacakes and chat.

"Good morning!" A young employee bounded up to them. She had a striped apron over her uniform of black t-shirt and tight jeans. She brandished a couple of menus. "Table for two?"

"We've come to see if Leon's available actually?" Trudy explained.

A brief moment of discombobulation passed over her face before she composed herself and invited them to take a seat whilst she went and fetched him.

"When was the last time you saw Leon?" Trudy asked her sister, as they waited in anticipation.

"Gawd," Maxine cast her mind back. She'd failed the eleven-plus, so didn't attend the Tolchester Grammar School like Trudy, Leon and Fiona. Her friends at secondary school were different from those she'd hung around with at primary school. "Probably the day of the quiz final. I'm expecting someone that still looks like this!"

She laid out the photograph onto the table in between them with a nervous giggle.

After a few minutes, their waitress re-emerged from a door behind the counter, a man in tow. He was as bulky as a rugby player, his rounded face decorated with an impressive bushy blond beard. He looked like a Viking. His striped apron matched that of the waitress, but the strings strained around his waist. Despite the vast alteration of appearance, the twinkling blue eyes and relaxed smile confirmed to the girls that this was Leon. As he approached their table, unrecognising, a familiar blush spread across his cheeks.

"Hi, I'm Leon. You wanted to see me?"

Trudy leaped to her feet, unsure whether to shake his hand, or hug him. She did neither. "It's Trudy and Maxine. From school..."

His eyes widened and he peered closer at the pair before remembering his manners. "Gosh, of course! Wow, it's been years...er, how are you both?"

He was clearly wondering what the hell they were doing in his café, and what they wanted from him, so Maxine was keen to move on from the small talk.

"Yeah, we're good. Sorry to land on you unannounced but we've come to put a proposition to you. Do you have a spare minute?"

Leon looked momentarily flustered, but confirmed that he did, and dispatched the waitress to fetch them a pot of tea and some cakes, whilst he took the seat between the twins. "I can't remember the last time I saw you," he confessed.

"We were just talking about that," Trudy replied. "I think I saw you on the beach a few years after we left school, but Maxine's not seen you since the quiz final in London."

"I didn't go to Tolchester Grammar like you," Maxine added defensively, "and then I left Clover Bay to go to university, and have barely came back here since. Well, only to visit Trudy."

Leon looked from Maxine to Trudy, and marvelled at how strange it was to see childhood friends as adults. Maxine's long rust-coloured hair was still her striking feature, and she'd been lucky enough to retain the slim athletic figure of her youth. But thirty years on, her face hadn't escaped the crinkles of time, no matter how expensive her moisturiser was.

Trudy had changed more, he decided. Not necessarily in a bad way, just more rounded, more mumsy.

Leon spotted the photo on the table and picked it up with a grin. "Did you bring this to remind yourself what I looked like?" He laughed. "Look at us. We were so bloody young!" He glanced down at his belly. "And skinny!"

The waitress approached with their tea and decanted the pot, cups and an array of small cakes from the tray onto the table. With a curious nod, she departed.

"That photo was taken in June 1981, so this summer will be the 30th anniversary," explained Maxine. "I had this idea, which might be mad, to reunite the gang in London to recreate the picture thirty years on."

There was no reaction from Leon, who continued to study the picture in thoughtful silence.

"The trophy's still on display in the school cabinet apparently," Trudy chipped in. "My husband works at Clover Bay Primary and is going to ask if we can borrow it for the photo. You know, if we do pull this thing off. He's trying to track down Miss Earle too."

"So, what does Fiona say? Has she agreed?" he said finally.

"We haven't had chance to track her down yet," Maxine admitted sheepishly.

"And what about Jayne?"

"Likewise, but we thought we'd start with you."

Leon continued to stare at the picture. The girls had expected him to jump at the opportunity but there was a definite hesitation. Maxine poured out the teas to break the silence.

"If we do this, I guess I'd have to take a day off to go to London," he mused. "This place is a seven-days-a-week operation so it's difficult to leave it." He placed the photo back down on the table between them and reached for a muffin.

"I'm sure you could be spared for one day," pleaded Trudy. "Is there a Mrs Batty who could hold the fort?"

"How do you plan to find Fiona and Jayne?" Leon replied, avoiding the question of Mrs Batty. As kids, they'd always joked that he'd never find anyone to marry him with that surname. No-one wanted to be Mrs Batty, did they? Looking around now at the vast farm shop and buzzing café, Maxine knew he'd make a great catch, despite his name.

"We haven't really started to look for them yet..." admitted Trudy.

"Well," Leon heaved himself to his feet. "Let me go and grab my laptop and we can start with a bit of Facebook stalking."

6

The book was getting exciting. Danny and his father waited as the pheasants all rose to the treetops to sleep, and the first few were beginning to drop to the ground as the effect of the sleeping pills took hold. Trudy was enthralled. What a clever way to collect up the birds so that Mr Hazell's shooting party would be sabotaged.

A shadow fell over the page and Trudy looked up in irritation. Jayne stood, hovering over her, resting her foot on the bottom of the steps where Trudy sat. This was her lunchtime refuge, behind the annexe that jutted out, and few people ever found her here as she read in peace.

"What book is that?" Jayne asked.

"Danny the Champion of the World," replied Trudy, flicking the cover up for her to see. She tried to keep the impatience from her voice. They would be called in from break in ten minutes, and she wanted to find out whether Danny and his father collected up all the pheasants in time.

"You're always reading," Jayne observed. It wasn't a criticism, but Trudy sensed it wasn't a compliment either.

"I like reading."

"Oh."

Without being invited, Jayne swung around and placed her bum on the step next to Trudy. "Have you read 'Anne of Green Gables'?" She chirped. "That's what I'm reading at the moment. It's about a girl who's got red hair - a bit like your sister - except that she's an orphan and gets sent off to live with..."

"No, I've not read it," Trudy interrupted. She placed her bookmark carefully at the right page and closed her book. She clearly wasn't going to be left to read in peace, and Roald Dahl would have to wait until she got home.

"It's set in Canada, where my mum is from. Well, the town in the book is made up, but my mum says that there's this place called New London where the author is from, and everyone thinks the book is set there, so all the tourists come and visit."

"A bit like Clover Bay in the summer, then," Trudy grinned. "It gets full of old people on their holidays. Although I don't think any books have been set here. It's far too boring."

The girls sat in silence for a few moments before Jayne turned to look at Trudy.

"Are you free on Saturday?" she asked.

Trudy shrugged. She'd like to finish her book, obviously. "I think so."

"Good. My mum has suggested the quiz team get together to practice some questions, and says you can all come to our house if you like. You can stay for supper."

A pulse of excitement shot through Trudy. She'd heard people in her parents' pub talk of the amazing house on the cliffs, and she never imagined she would get an invite to such a cool place.

Jayne stood up and smoothed down her skirt. She sensed they would be called back to the classroom soon. "I hope Fiona and Leon can come. It'll be fun."

"Can Maxine join us?" Trudy asked, praying that Jayne would say yes. "She's not on the quiz team but Miss Earle wants her to be the lucky charm, so she should be part of the group."

In reality, Trudy didn't want to face the inevitable tantrum if she were to be excluded. She studied Jayne's face, where a flicker of hesitation crossed her features.

"Yeah, of course." Jayne didn't see the point in Maxine coming. She wasn't part of the quiz team so wouldn't be able to answer any of their test questions, but maybe they could make her the quizmaster.

Fiona was thrilled to be asked, especially to have the invite extended to an evening meal. A Saturday tea in the Farr household usually meant toast. If she was lucky there would be a can of beans and mini sausages in the cupboard that she could share with her older brother, Darryl. She knew that Jayne's parents would serve something better than beans and mini sausages on toast.

The four classmates agreed to meet up on the seafront and head up to Jayne's house together. It was a blustery October Saturday, and the promenade was quiet as the gang gathered. Leon had pedalled the two miles from the farm on his cherry-red Chopper bike. It was his pride and joy, having received it last Christmas from his parents. The front forks were splattered with mud from the farm track, but Leon vowed to clean it on Sunday and keep it shiny. Trudy and Maxine lived closest to the seafront, so walked together, whilst Fiona journeyed in from the tower blocks in the valley on a battered skateboard that she'd stolen from Darryl. She had no idea where Darryl would have got it from. No doubt he would have nicked it off of one of the estate kids. It was a kind of sharing economy around their way. People took stuff from each other, but nobody could call the police because it had been stolen in the first place. Darryl was no exception, and Fiona feared for her brother's future. He hung around with the wrong crowd and wasn't bright enough to keep himself streetwise and not be taken advantage of. Fiona glanced around her school friends as she joined them and realised she was lucky. These were good people.

"I like your Chopper, Leon," Fiona observed. She had learned not to be jealous of what other people had. It did no good.

"It's fast," he enthused. "I got here in fifteen minutes," he added, checking his digital Casio calculator watch. It was his second most prized possession, bought with the money he'd saved from doing jobs around the farm combined with some birthday money from his grandmother.

"I'll race you to the whelk hut," Fiona challenged.

"You'll never beat me," he countered, but Fiona was already off, grabbing a short head start. The wheels rumbled over the cracks of the promenade as she powered off with a dogged determination.

"I bet I can beat both of them," Maxine told Trudy impulsively, setting off after the pair at a tenacious sprint. Trudy shrugged tolerantly, sauntering after them all at her own pace.

Leon pedalled furiously, Fiona crouched low as she pushed as hard as she could with her left foot to propel the creaky board forward, but the pair were astonished to experience Maxine overtake them, arms pumping, legs pounding as she approached her goal.

"Blimey Maxine," laughed Leon as she reached the tatty shack first. He didn't even care that Fiona had also reached the destination ahead of him. "You're fast!"

"Miss Earle thinks so too," she gloated, panting deep gulps of air into her lungs. "She thinks I could run for the big school when we go up next year."

The gang fell silent, allowing Maxine the small pleasure of winning the race. They crossed the small footbridge across the stream and headed along the lane out of Clover Bay. The blackberry bushes bulged into the road, although the autumn fruit had long gone. To the left they could hear the distant slap of waves against the sides the cliffs, but the surroundings were suddenly blissfully peaceful.

Leon began to puff as the incline took its toll on his legs, but he stood up on the pedals and powered ahead of the girls. Fiona gave up on the skateboard and tucked it under her arm, strolling alongside the twins.

"This is it!" Leon called to them, spotting the house ahead. "Wait for me while I lock my bike up. My mum will go mad if it gets stolen."

"I don't think people around here nick things," Fiona observed, looking at the vast green fields. Nevertheless, Leon studiously extracted his lock from his rucksack and chained the bike's frame to the gatepost at the entrance to Jayne's house.

"It's big, isn't it?" Trudy observed, looking at the unusual structure of wood and glass that lay at the end of the gravel driveway.

"It's weird," added Fiona. The houses around her estate were all packed in tightly. Entire streets of identical, neglected, squat and boxy houses lined scruffy, littered roads. This house stood proudly at the end of its manicured surroundings. There was no chance there would ever be an abandoned fridge on the front lawn here, nor a battered, rusty wheel-less car resting on bricks like her neighbour had.

The gang traipsed up the gravel path to the enormous wood panelled front door where Leon rang the doorbell. The austere clang inside could be heard through the thick door. After a few minutes, the door swung inwards and a man greeted them, smiling broadly in welcome. He wore jeans and a checked shirt, with a baseball cap pulled low to his eyebrows.

"Hi guys. You must be here to see Jayne." His accent was different. He sounded like he should be in a movie. He stepped sideways and indicated that they should enter. The friends stepped over the threshold and found themselves in a vast, airy hallway. The walls were bare wood, but the expansive windows let light pour in. A warm aroma of baking hung in the air. "There's a closet here if you want to leave any coats, or things. Is that a skateboard?" he asked Fiona. "That's real neat!"

Before Fiona could reply, a petite lady emerged from a side door, wiping flour from her hands onto the loud, floral apron that covered her front. "Welcome, guys!" She echoed her husband, and smiled at the group, swiftly appraising them. "Jayne! Your friends are here," she hollered into the house. "I'm just making some buns," she explained. Fiona desperately hoped they were destined for the quiz team as she was starving. She hadn't had breakfast as Darryl had used up all the milk and the last few slices of bread had green patches of mould in the centre. Fiona had thrown them in the bin, and realised that her mum was nowhere to be seen and there wasn't any loose change laying around the house for her to take to the corner shop.

Jayne appeared with a self-conscious wave at the gang. "Give your friends a tour, honey," her mum encouraged, "whilst I finish the buns and your dad can set up the quiz".

They followed Jayne through from the hallway to the back of the house, which was one open-plan room. The far end of the room was entirely glass panelled, giving a vista over the green lawn, which dropped away at the cliff edge to the angry grey waves of the sea beyond. Adults always gushed over the scale of the room, and even as ten-year-olds, the friends could appreciate that this wasn't an ordinary house. Jayne explained that her dad was an architect and had designed this house and had it built from scratch. "It's on a two-acre plot," she continued like an estate agent, "so we've divided up the land and created some paddocks and stabling for our horses, but left the other side of the house wild. There are so many brambles we just left it. In the summer the blackberries were growing faster than we could pick them. The freezer is full of blackberry crumble". Fiona wondered whether she would be allowed to take one home with her. She'd give her right arm for a blackberry crumble.

The open-plan living area was sectioned up using the furniture as a guide to the function of the space. On one side, oversized squishy sofas formed a U-shape around a large fireplace. In the centre of the room was a long oak dining table. Maxine counted ten chairs around the table, which seemed excessive for a family of four. The kitchen took up the other end, where Mrs Gray was fussing around with the oven.

"Don't you have a TV?" Leon questioned, looking around the room.

"Yes, it's in the den," Jayne replied, waving them over to a set of stairs that descended to a basement area below the main living space. Jayne flicked on a light, as the subterranean space lacked the natural light enjoyed by the rest of the house.

"Whoa!" gasped Leon. His eyes fell first on the table football, then scanned around to see another set of inviting settees that faced the TV set. Beyond that there was a dartboard on the wall and a pinball machine. "Do you have to put money in to play pinball?" He walked over to the table football and instinctively spun the rods to make the plastic players somersault. "Can we have a game?"

Jayne looked doubtful. "Let's see if we have time. I have to show you the rest of the house, and then we need to do some quiz questions and my mum's making buns…"

Reluctantly they followed Jayne back up the stairs, all silently preferring to spend the afternoon playing downstairs in the den than answering questions. They were shown the upstairs next. The bathroom was warm and luxurious and contained a bathtub the size of Fiona's kitchen. They continued along the landing. "We can't go in there. It's my sister's room, and she's very protective of it." The door was shut and, to reinforce the message, had a sign saying KEEP OUT swinging on the handle. Jayne's room faced out over the garden, and was so tidy. Trudy wondered whether she had spent the whole morning clearing up, or whether Jayne was obsessively neat. She inspected the bookcase and realised that the paperbacks were sorted in alphabetical order by author. That gave her the answer.

"I have all sorts of games in my closet," Jayne opened up the white Louvre doors to reveal neat shelves lined with board games. "We can play some games later if we have time."

"Can we see your horse?" Fiona asked. "I love horses."

"Oh yeah, of course. Do you ride?"

Fiona smiled sagely. The price of lessons was way out of her mum's reach. "Not really, but I'd love to learn."

She hoped Jayne might take the hint. It would be no skin off Jayne's nose to let her have a few rides on her pony, surely? They followed Jayne back down the stairs and through a side door that led to a path to the paddock. A jet-black pony with a bushy mane stood chomping contentedly at the grass. Beyond that stood a shiny chestnut with a uniform white blaze down his nose. "This one is mine," she explained, clicking her tongue to make the black horse saunter over to the fence. "She's called Beauty. You know, as in Black Beauty."

Fiona stroked the pony's nose and was fascinated as it wobbled its lips towards her.

"That pony over there is Bella, and she belongs to my sister, Nina," Jayne explained. Bella lifted her head and inspected the gang before ambling off in the opposite direction, unimpressed. It seemed as though Bella was as sociable as Jayne's sister, Nina.

"You should offer up the ponies to the school for their summer fete," Trudy suggested. "Let the public have pony rides to raise some money."

"That's a great idea," enthused Fiona, whose only thought was that it provided an opportunity for a free ride. If not entirely gratis, then even a mate's rate now that she and Jayne were friends?

"Maybe." Jayne didn't seem convinced. She turned from the fence and indicated that they should follow her back indoors. Fiona gave Beauty one last pat and begrudgingly followed her friends.

There wasn't time for adventure in the den that afternoon, nor even a play on any of the board games in Jayne's neat pile. All the gang would admit that they had fun, though, with Jayne's dad having compiled all the quiz questions on scraps of paper and set up the quiz environment on a long table in the dining area. He'd rated each question a different amount of points according to its difficulty, so Maxine felt elated with importance when her role as quizmaster included not only reading the questions out, but chalking up the scores on a large blackboard that Jayne's dad had prepared for the occasion.

"I've even got you each a kind of buzzer," he explained to the four contestants. The engineering side of Mr Gray had gone into overdrive in preparation for the quiz, and he'd adapted four doorbells to make different noises so that Maxine could tell who had buzzed. There was even a procedure in place where Maxine had to announce the surname of the contestant who buzzed first before they could offer their answer. If they got it wrong, points were deducted.

Mr Gray hung around on the sidelines to act as adjudicator when things went wrong. A few disputes erupted over who had pressed their buzzer first, or whether the answer on Maxine's piece of paper was wrong. Her arithmetic even led to a dressing down from Trudy, when she calculated the points incorrectly.

Mrs Gray spent the afternoon fussing in the kitchen area, but had an ear over the proceedings. Every now and again she would call out an encouragement, like "Great job!" or "Excellent answer!" before turning her attention back to the stove.

There was a half time break for the promised buns, during which Mr Gray took it upon himself to have a team talk. The tactics with the school quiz competitions was for each member to have specialised subjects that they could revise for, he advised. "Leon, you're clearly strong on science, astronomy and history. Trudy, you're getting all the questions right on art and literature. Jayne, you're great on geography, sport and animals, whilst Fiona... well, you know a little bit about a lot. Kind of a strange array of knowledge you've got, haven't you?"

She supposed he was right. She liked to watch John Craven's Newsround most days and tried to engage Darryl or her mum in debate about some of the things she heard. She knew that when people spoke about "Maggie" they were talking about Margaret Thatcher. It seemed that she was a trouble maker and didn't do anything for the likes of her and the people on her estate. The unemployment was rising out of control, and inflation was getting high, although Fiona was yet to understand what that meant. She finally asked her mum, who explained that it was "when something that cost a bloody fortune yesterday now cost even more of a bloody fortune today".

On the TV news, she had watched Maggie, the prime minister, giving her speech at the party conference. Fiona found herself in awe at the way she oozed confidence, but felt conflicted, knowing she wasn't supposed to like The Iron Lady, as she was becoming known. The audience at the conference roared with appreciation at her speech, standing and clapping for several minutes when she finished. "Bunch of bloody rich toffs, the Conservatives," had been Darryl's assessment when Fiona asked him what he thought. "They now say that we - as council house tenants - have the right to buy our homes. Oh, thanks a lot. With what? We can barely afford to buy a loaf of sodding bread."

She remembered Darryl's words as she took another look around the Gray's impressive open-plan living space. No such worries for them. The world was truly divided and the likes of her would never have the opportunity to be anything but a product of her background.

7

Leon returned from the office with his laptop and sat between the twins. As hordes of customers around them continued to natter and indulge in carrot cake and tea, he launched the browser and waited for Facebook to load.

"Are you on here?" he asked the pair.

"I am, just to keep in touch with book group and school things," Trudy replied. "I don't use it much, though."

"No, not me," Maxine replied apologetically. "I'm not really into that social networking side." In reality, her husband Grant didn't approve of such websites, and although she would admit it to nobody, he forbade her from creating a profile. She had been tempted to, especially with him being out of the house most of the week. She figured he wouldn't find out, but decided it wasn't worth the risk. He'd warned of fraudsters getting your details and clearing out your bank accounts, or stealing your identity and committing crimes in your name. She wasn't that bothered, she convinced herself.

"Right, well, I'll start with befriending you, Trudy..." Leon clicked around the site.

"Easton," Trudy corrected him, as he started to type in her maiden name.

"You married Jason Easton!" He chuckled, as the profile picture of Trudy and Jason grinning at the camera came onto the screen. "He hasn't changed a bit."

Having sent the friend request to Trudy, he turned his attention to the search for the missing quiz team. It was a nuisance that people on Facebook tended to use their married names. If Fiona and Jayne were married then the chances of finding them could be slim.

He started with Jayne. "Oh my God, there are hundreds of Jayne Grays." He started to scan through the list, muttering eliminating details about them as he went. "Works at Bolton College, no, retired, no, black, no, educated at the Johannesburg Educational Centre, no, likes boxing... can't see that myself." He sighed, but carried on scrolling silently, scrutinising profile pictures as he went.

"How about searching for her sister instead? Wasn't she called Nina? That's a less common name," suggested Trudy.

"Good shout," praised Leon, typing "Nina Gray" into the search box. "Hmmm, there's quite a lot of these too. I'm not sure I'd recognise her unless she kept the same haircut, which is unlikely."

It was true; her haircut had been a defining feature. Cropped short enough to earn her a place in the army, Nina's hair always appeared as fierce as her scowling features. Leon scrolled through the pictures slowly, screwing up his eyes trying to recognise any glimpse of 1981 in their features. The task seemed fruitless.

"Let's try Fiona," urged Maxine, getting despondent with the lack of success finding Jayne. "Farr," she prompted, seeing that Leon's memory was struggling.

They waited as he inputted the name and a small list of names appeared.

"Not many of these…" he peered closer at the screen. "Not that one." He dismissed the profile picture of a lady in her seventies. "That one's too young," he rejected the pouting blonde starlet with oversized lips. "Here's one with a profile picture of a cat. Do we think Fiona was a cat person?"

The girls shrugged. Thirty years could change a person - especially one that had barely time to establish an adult personality when they last saw her. Leon clicked into the profile. "Went to East Richland High School, no, that's not her."

"She's probably on her fourth marriage by now. She was the one who was voted the biggest slag in our year at secondary school," Trudy offered up unkindly.

"Well, the only other one is Fiona Farr-Foxham," Leon pointed out. They leaned in to view the profile picture of a brunette in her late teens or early twenties, resplendent in a floaty summer dress, standing on the edge of a marina. The blue sky and spotless white yachts provided a backdrop as perfect as her wide smile. The photo was clearly not of Fiona, but the girl could be the right age for a daughter.

They scanned the profile, but there were few details. "She checked into Pizza Express in Kensington six months ago, she's had a profile picture of a bunch of flowers previously, and it says she lives in Kent."

"What about her friends? Perhaps there's some mutual friends we recognise?" suggested Trudy.

Leon nodded his approval and clicked on the link to display her friend list. No mutual friends, and the ones she had was a short list of other Foxhams, and people with connections to London, and Kent.

"Well, I guess we could send her a message. No harm in asking if it's her."

Five minutes later, Leon had clicked the send button and there was nothing further they could do but wait. The girls swapped mobile numbers with Leon so that they could keep up to date, and they all agreed to have a think about what else they could do to track down Jayne.

"What do we do if we draw a blank on both Fiona and Jayne? It'll make a pretty crap photo with just me and Leon," Trudy confessed as the sisters clambered back into her car. They were satiated with tea and cake, elated with Leon's reaction to the project, but frustrated at the lack of progress finding fifty percent of the quiz team. Maxine prayed this wasn't all going to be a waste of time.

"Let's cross that bridge when we get to it," Maxine soothed in reply. "Now, what shall we do for the rest of the day?"

They arrived back at Lennox Street five hours later, having parked in town for an amble along the deserted beach before eating fish and chips out of the greasy paper on a bench on the harbourside. The tangy stench of fish arose from the trawler boats bobbing on the tide, whilst excited seagulls swooped overhead, squabbling with their piercing squawks. The air was still icy as the February temperature hadn't risen much above freezing all day.

"It feels like we're bunking off school," Trudy observed, scrunching up her chip paper. There was a glisten of grease across her lips. "Normally on a day off from work I'd be doing housework, or food shopping, or catching up on reading for my book club."

Maxine was amazed that anyone read anything for a book club. She thought the social occasion was just an excuse for girls to get together and sink a bottle of wine.

"We could always see what's on at the cinema. That'll warm us up," Maxine suggested. "I remember bunking off school to go and see Gremlins with Wayne Ford. We were shitting ourselves about being asked for ID as it was a 15 certificate and neither of us were old enough." She smiled at the memory. "I bet The Regal is still a flea pit, isn't it?"

"Nope," replied Trudy. "It closed down about ten years ago, but there's a multiplex on the edge of Tolchester."

So, three hours and a carton of popcorn later, the girls arrived back having sat through an animated film based on Romeo and Juliet. It was enjoyable escapism with a few laughs for the sisters.

"Where have you two been?" Jason asked, turning from the sink as they shuffled through the hallway. It wasn't an accusation; he was genuinely interested. They took a seat at the kitchen table and Trudy filled him in on their day whilst Maxine marvelled at Jason's ability to be helpful in the kitchen. He'd cleaned up all the breakfast debris and had made a start on Robbie's sandwiches for his lunch the next day. Grant barely stepped foot in the kitchen, Maxine reflected. Sometimes when they had friends over, he claimed he played his part by keeping the guests entertained and their drinks topped up, whilst Maxine cooked, tidied or loaded the dishwasher.

"Well, I've had a breakthrough," Jason grinned. "Wait there..." He disappeared into the hallway and rifled in his work bag. When he returned, he brandished the hefty gold trophy that had proudly taken centre stage in the school cabinet for the past 30 years. "Ta-dah!"

Trudy took the trophy from him and regarded it fondly. The heavy black marble base had a brass plaque on the front, and the engraving confirmed that Clover Bay Primary were quiz champions in 1981. Coming off the base was a golden scroll, with two fat question marks in relief. The last time the sisters had seen that trophy was the summer of 1981 when they left the primary school to start the next chapters in their lives.

"You obviously have to take good care of that and return it after the photo," Jason said needlessly.

"Of course," agreed Trudy.

"Mr Riley was really enthusiastic about the photo when I told him," Jason explained. "He was around at the time. Do you remember him? He used to have a dodgy mullet and got us running around in the rain all the time? Anyway, he's the head teacher now," he said for Maxine's benefit, "and said we should do a press release to publicise the photo".

"It's not really that newsworthy, is it?" questioned Maxine in horror. When she first had the idea, she just imagined having a nice day in London catching up with old friends.

"Mr Riley seems to think so. Better still, he's still in touch with Miss Earle, and is going to contact her to see whether she'd be interested in getting involved."

"My God, that's brilliant!" Trudy gasped. She rose from her seat and pecked Jason on the cheek gratefully. "This has the potential to be epic."

"Excellent!" echoed Maxine, her stomach flipping with excitement. What on earth would Miss Earle be like thirty years on?

8

The weather was starting to take a turn for the better, which pleased Fiona, who couldn't bare those icy Nordic winds that had been slicing across the country for most of February. She woke in a contented mood and, as she pulled back the bedroom curtain, enjoyed the sensation of the morning sun illuminating her face. It felt as though spring was on the way and soon the cherry blossom trees would burst into colour, providing the splash of pink to contrast against the vast green lawn.

The other source of her serenity today was knowing that Fortuna was coming for lunch. She didn't see as much of her daughter as she would have liked, especially as the 40-minute train journey between them wasn't a barrier, but Fiona knew that the thrill of life in London was a bigger magnet than coming back to Kent to have lunch with her boring old mum. She was appreciative that Fortuna worked hard for the family business, putting in endless hours, including at the weekends, and that her role took priority over coming home to the nest. But it would be nice to be more involved in her life.

She paused by Fortuna's bedroom on her way to head downstairs. It remained just the way Fortuna left it when she made the move to London a year ago. Her clothes still hung in the wardrobe and there was a bombsite of make-up strewn across her dressing table. On the rare occasions that Fortuna came home for the weekend, it was handy to have everything there waiting for her, and on days like today when Fiona was feeling nostalgic, she could wander into the room and convince herself that she could smell Fortuna's Parisian perfume hanging in the air. Her feet led her into the room and she paused to gaze at the photos assembled in a collage in their frame to the side of the bed. Every picture brought back a memory. Fortuna looking resplendent on the marina at Portofino last summer. Fiona loved that picture so much that she had made it her profile picture on Facebook. It had been the only holiday that the two of them had been on together and it had been fabulous.

A picture of Ted took pride of place in the centre of the collage. It had been taken by Fortuna at a barbeque in the garden on one of those balmy summer evenings, Ted wearing his favourite apron that asked "Who wants my sausage?" He was brandishing a pair of tongs in one hand and a glass of amber beer in the other, grinning with pleasure.

There was a group shot of Fortuna with a gaggle of school friends, arms around each other, grinning at each other, and Fiona appeared in a shot taken on the seafront at Clover Bay. The faded colours on the picture indicated its age, taken in the mid-80s when Fiona was still a teenager. Oh my, she thought sadly, I'll be 41 this year. Where did the years go?

After breakfasting, she turned her attention to her voluntary job with the local animal rescue centre. It was a grassroots charity that started with a couple who couldn't resist getting involved when a cat or dog needed a new loving home. Over the past two decades they had extended their garden to provide a cattery, kennels, and now even a rented paddock for donkeys and ponies. Fiona began volunteering when Fortuna started secondary school and her empty days needed filling. She created a veg patch in the garden and grew salads to help feed the rabbits and guinea pigs, and carrots for the horses and ponies. As she became more integrated into the charity, Fiona learnt to update the website, taking photos of the animals and creating their stories online. This morning she was going to feature Mr Tuna as Cat of the Week. The fluffy ginger's owner had sadly had to move into a hospice and he needed a new forever home.

She switched on the computer in the study and went to the email to see if there was anything in the inbox that needed her attention first. Deleting the spam and junk that had accumulated since she last logged on a couple of days ago, her attention was drawn to a notification from Facebook that a new chat message awaited her. She was expecting the message to relate to the numerous groups she dabbled in, either the rescue centre, the parish council, or the fans of the local pub, but no. This was a message to her personally. From Leon Batty. Thankfully you don't forget a name like Leon Batty and she didn't have to delve too far into her creaking memory to place him.

"Hello, I'm wondering if you are the Fiona Farr that went to school in Clover Bay," the message read. "If so, I'm hoping you'd be interested in getting together with me and the twins (Trudy and Maxine) to recreate the photo from 1981 of us with the quiz trophy in London. Please get in touch! PS: If you're not the right Fiona Farr then sorry to have bothered you." He'd left an email address.

Fiona's heart was pounding. She hadn't given the quiz team from thirty years ago a thought since she left Clover Bay in 1986. Of course, she'd promised to keep in touch as she waved farewell to Trudy and took her array of O-Levels to London as her mum relocated with the new love of her life. But once settled into the new rhythm of the big city, sleepy Clover Bay seemed like a different lifetime and her pledge to remain connected to her friends crumbled.

She read the message again. Leon, Trudy and Maxine. What about Jayne? No mention of Jayne.

It would be interesting to discover what they had all become, she mused. It would also surprise them to learn that Fiona hadn't trodden the same path as her mother. Whilst she was technically a single parent, she was a widow, left with a bright, intelligent daughter and a comfortable lifestyle in suburban Kent.

Curiosity drove her to glimpse Leon's profile, and she gasped with surprise at his bushy beard and fuller figure. He'd always been so scrawny in his youth. There wasn't much information on his profile except that he still cited Clover Bay as his hometown.

Hesitantly she typed Jayne Gray's name into the search box, but as Leon had discovered, there were far too many to be able to identify the fourth member of the quiz team. Fiona felt apprehensive thinking about Jayne. It had taken her a long time after the Gray family's sudden disappearance to stop feeling guilty that it was somehow her fault. Inexplicably, nearly thirty years on, those feelings bubbled away again in the pit of her stomach. Had they found Jayne? Would Jayne want to be part of a reunion? Could she face her again?

In Clover Bay, Fiona had clung onto Jayne like a limpet in an attempt to get more involved with her horses. She cast her mind back and remembered the day that she had gate-crashed the trip to the pony club show. She blushed at the memory.

"Can I come with you?" Fiona had asked bluntly when Jayne let slip that her Saturday was taken up with competing in the Tolchester pony club events.

"Oh, I... er..." Jayne was temporarily flummoxed as she looked into Fiona's dark pleading eyes. "We won't be able to give you a lift because we're all going and there's quite a lot of gear, and it's cramped in the car."

Fiona's face fell with disappointment but when she got home that evening and moaned about the predicament to her mum, she was amazed to be offered a lift.

"You'll have to get yourself home, though," her mum negotiated, "as I've got too much else to be doing than ferrying you around, but the bus goes twice an hour."

When Fiona pulled back her curtains that Saturday morning, her heart sank as wispy grey clouds hung in the air and squally showers swept across the rolling green hills on the horizon. Tolchester sat just beyond the ridge in the distance, and she knew it was going to be dismal weather all day.

She tugged on Darryl's flared jeans that he'd outgrown, and tightened the baggy waist with an old belt she found in the back of his wardrobe. She wished she owned a pair of jodhpurs, then she would look the part amongst all the riders today, but the best she could manage was jeans and an old sweatshirt. She didn't have a pair of Wellington boots, so hoped her trainers would stand up to the muddy conditions. She pulled on her cagoule. It was the most waterproof coat she owned, but inconveniently not very warm. She was willing to risk getting cold for staying dry.

"I'll drop you off here as I'm going to see Angie," her mum said, pulling into a bus stop on the edge of Tolchester. "You can walk the rest, can't you?"

Fiona knew better than to protest. It wasn't far to cut across a couple of fields, and safer than negotiating the country lane that accessed the show.

She could see horseboxes turning down the track, and used the glimpses of them to direct her towards the entrance. The field she traversed was already boggy from the persistent drizzle and her toes felt the first signs of dampness creeping through her socks. Well, she told herself, if you want to be a horsewoman you have to tolerate all weather conditions.

She had no idea whether it would cost anything to enter the show ground. She only possessed the bus fare home, so paying to get into the event wasn't an option. As she approached, she hovered by the gate opposite to watch what happened as the horseboxes entered, and was perturbed to see a woman approach the driver's window, exchange some words and pass some papers through the gap. Fiona pulled her dripping hood lower over her face and strode confidently alongside the horsebox where she was shielded from view of the woman. As the horsebox pulled forward, she carried on walking in time to the vehicle and arrived in the showground unseen by officials. She grinned at her small victory, and started the hunt for the Gray family.

She squelched over to the main arena, where the show jumps were laid out ready for competition. It was still early and, although many competitors had arrived, nothing was yet underway.

The catering vans were setting up, the hum of their generators teasing that there would soon be aromas of chips, and hot dogs and doughnuts drifting from their interiors.

Beyond the vans she discovered a roped off practice area containing a couple of jumps. They were more basic than the colourful poles in the main arena, but performed the same function. Fiona had the urge to run into the zone, mimicking the gait of a cantering horse and jump the practice obstacle with a whack of an invisible whip on her thigh. She restrained herself and continued to traverse the field.

All the horseboxes were lined up in the side field and Fiona paused to watch as ponies were decanted from them. The junior members of the pony club were all smartly dressed in their clean jodhpurs, with shiny black riding boots and waxed jackets that repelled the droplets from the rain. They proudly tethered their mounts and began the process of getting them ready for competition.

A hundred metres up the row was the familiar figure of Jayne, leading Beauty out of the box, and it was all Fiona could do to stop herself sprinting up to her.

"Hi Jayne," she greeted as casually as she could, arriving alongside the vehicle.

"Oh!" Jayne looked surprised, but quickly found her manners. "You made it."

"Yeah, my mum was coming this way so dropped me off." She stepped forward and patted Beauty. Nina emerged from the horsebox leading Bella down the ramp. Fiona gave her a little wave, but Nina's weak smile in reply faded from her face within seconds.

"Hi Fiona!" Mrs Gray emerged from the car, tugging on an enormous wide-brimmed wax hat that shielded the rain from her torso. "We didn't know you were coming. We could have given you a lift."

Fiona glanced around to see whether Mr Gray was with them, but she couldn't see him. She turned her attention back to Jayne and Beauty.

"Can I do anything to help you?"

Jayne was bustling around, fetching a box of grooming tools from the car boot.

"I don't think so," Jayne replied. "I have to get Beauty ready for competition."

Fiona stepped aside as Jayne started to brush Beauty's coat vigorously. The pony was very docile.

"Would you like me to do the other side?" Fiona asked. She ached to have a brush in her hand and discover how it felt to have that closeness with such a lovely animal.

"Better not," Jayne replied dismissively. "You need a certain technique and both sides have to match."

"Oh." Fiona scrutinised Jayne's brushing style. It didn't look that specialist to her.

"You should have worn rubber boots," Jayne pointed out critically. Fiona looked down at her feet where her gym shoes were now saturated. Her feet felt numb.

"I didn't realise quite how wet it would be up here," Fiona lied.

Mrs Gray, ever the host, searched through every inch of the Land Rover to see whether there was any spare footwear that Fiona could borrow, but drew a blank.

"I'm fine," Fiona fibbed. The cold and wet would all be worthwhile if Jayne or Nina permitted her to have a sit on the ponies. Or even a brush.

She tried not to shiver as she stood watching the sisters as they cleaned out the ponies' hooves, plaited their manes and tails, and then tacked them up. Fiona soaked up every bit of the equine education.

"They never look as good in the rain," Mrs Gray observed. "But at least everyone's in the same boat."

"What time are you jumping?" Fiona asked, eager for some action.

"Not until this afternoon," Jayne replied, tugging on her riding hat. She pushed past Fiona to untie Beauty and mounted with the deftness of a gymnast.

"What do you do until then?" Fiona glanced at her watch. It was only eleven o'clock.

"I'll keep Beauty warm, take her for a bit of a hack, catch up with some other competitors, then do a bit of practice." She tapped her heels into Beauty's side and the pair started to move off. "I'll catch you later."

Fiona realised her mouth was hanging open, so she quickly shut it and smiled at the retreating backside. Nina had mounted Bella and waved farewell to her mother as she trotted after her sister.

"Well, it was lovely to see you again," said Mrs Gray, removing her sodden hat and clambering into the Land Rover. She picked up a magazine and positioned her glasses on her nose. "I hope you'll all come over for some more quiz practice soon."

"I'd love to," enthused Fiona. A shiver escaped her, and she bade farewell to Mrs Gray. Her presence was no longer welcome, that much was clear to the ten-year-old. She contemplated watching the show jumping that had commenced, but in truth she was chilled to the core, and her legs were aching from standing all morning. She realised that there was nothing to do but head for home.

9

"So, we've left a message for the most likely Fiona Farr," Maxine explained to Grant that Friday night as they sat at the kitchen island, tucking into a lasagne that Maxine had spent all afternoon perfecting. Grant had once said that his mother made the best lasagne in the world, so Maxine was tenacious in her pursuit for the perfect rival to his mother's. "We're not sure whether it's her or not," she continued. "This Fiona Farr has a double-barrelled surname, which doesn't sound likely for the Fiona Farr we knew at school."

"No?"

"No," Maxine replied with a smile. "That's what posh people do, isn't it, when two great families come together." The more she thought about it, the less likely it seemed that they had tracked down the correct Fiona Farr. "Despite going to the grammar school, Fiona was secretly voted the most likely girl in secondary school to get up the duff before her O-Levels, and her brother was most likely to be in prison before he was eighteen. It was that sort of family, if you know what I mean."

Grant grinned. He knew some people from school that earned those labels from the other kids. He reached for the wine bottle and topped their glasses up before turning his attention back to his lasagne.

"And did the prophecies come true?"

Maxine shook her head and took a sip of wine. "Trudy heard that her brother joined the army, which was probably the best place for him. And to her credit, Fiona managed to get her O-Levels before any impregnating that we knew of, but she moved to London soon after so anything could have happened to her beyond that point."

Grant placed his cutlery down on his empty plate and pushed it away from him. He looked at Maxine curiously. "And what did the kids secretly vote as most likely for you to do?"

"Don't know," she replied with a shrug. "Most likely to end up in the Olympics, or something to do with my running, I suppose."

41

Grant reached across and took her hand in a rare act of affection. "Not most likely to marry the greatest catch of the East Midlands then?"

She smiled back at him. She had been lucky, she knew that. They had met at a gym, although neither knew from that first encounter that there would be a lifetime together from there. Twenty-two-year-old Maxine had been running on a treadmill, minding her own business. She preferred to run outside, but the January ice conspired against her plans, and so she diverted to the gym on the outskirts of Loughborough. Housed in a converted warehouse, it was shabby on the outside and male dominated on the inside. The body builders hogged the free weights, whilst teenagers that were inspired by Chris Eubank smacked the numerous punch bags in the middle of the gym floor. Down the far end was a line of treadmills, rowing machines and steppers facing the windows that looked out over an uninspiring, grey trading estate.

Maxine was on her fifth mile when a man stepped onto the treadmill next to her. He glanced across and smiled amiably before pressing his start button and increasing his speed. Maxine was running at her cruising speed of six miles an hour, but when the man set his speed at six and a half miles per hour, the competitive side of Maxine kicked in and she increased her speed to seven miles per hour.

After thirty seconds she saw her neighbour nudge his speed up to seven and a half miles an hour. She looked across at him. He looked straight back at her, challenging with his baby blue eyes. He had an athletic build, but not enough to intimidate Maxine.

She knew where her limits were and there was plenty of speed left in her legs yet. She turned up the speed to eight miles an hour. The man matched her speed and they paced wordlessly in unison for a couple of minutes. Maxine could sense the man getting out of breath. Time for the kill. She flicked her speed up to ten miles per hour and looked over at him, laying down the dare.

He increased his speed to match hers, but as the seconds ticked by he was losing the battle to maintain his dignity as his lungs cried for more air. He finally stabbed at the emergency stop button on his panel and, as his floor stopped rotating, he bent double, fighting to get his breath on an even keel.

Serenely Maxine reduced her speed back down to six miles an hour and she nodded at him to acknowledge her triumph. He smiled back in defeat and her stomach flipped. He gave a brief wave of farewell and staggered off across the gym floor and she presumed she would never see him again.

At the time she was still living in the same property that she had resided in during her final years of university. It was a dated Victorian house in Exeter Terrace that had a bathtub in the cramped kitchen, which doubled up as the worktop. Needless to say, the students never took a bath; nobody wanted to be naked in the kitchen. There was no bathroom; just a toilet on the middle floor with two roomy bedrooms, and a generous attic room at the top of the house. As a result of its frugality, the rent was ridiculously cheap and she had got used to using the shower at the gym, or local swimming pool. She shared the house with Jessie and Clarky. Her university housemates had moved on after graduation and the landlord, Mr Khan, a gentle, kind family man, had advertised for new tenants and brought in two new housemates that Maxine barely saw. Jessie worked for the police and, between unsociable shift patterns, an exhausting and complicated social life and lots of sleeping, their paths barely crossed. Clarky was a quiet, studious lad who worked long hours in the lab at the hospital, then spent most evenings watching Star Trek in his bedroom.

It made Maxine jump when he spoke to her as she heated up baked beans on the stove one evening.

"So, Mr Khan came to collect the rent this morning, but he says he's got to move back to Pakistan. Some family matters."

"Oh?"

"The bad news is that he's not planning to return to the UK, so says he needs to sell the house. He doesn't know if the new owner will continue to rent it out, or want us gone."

This bombshell made Maxine fear the worst. If the buyer wanted to end their tenancies, she would have to find somewhere else to live and there were few opportunities for paying as little rent in Loughborough as she did in Exeter Terrace. She had no choice but to sit it out, waiting to discover what course of action the new landlord would take.

The last person she expected to find on the doorstep a few weeks later was the challenger from the gym. He didn't recognise her at first as he introduced himself as Grant Carver, and, as soon-to-be owner of the house, he had popped around to meet the residents. It wasn't until Maxine invited him in and offered him a drink that he narrowed his eyes and tilted his head.

"Have we met before?" he ventured.

"I think I may have outrun you on the treadmill at the gym," she confirmed.

He blushed and nodded, the recollection coming back to him. He leaned on the doorframe of the kitchen as she made coffee. She was convinced he was watching her, as many men did, but he later admitted to appraising the kitchen. His brain never stopped looking at the potential of spaces, and this dated example was begging to be ripped out and given the Carver treatment.

"I cannot believe there's a bath in the kitchen," he commented.

"We don't use it, for obvious reasons," Maxine replied, handing him his mug of coffee. Their eyes locked momentarily. It was almost like the challenge in the gym again, only this time Maxine was challenging him to threaten her with eviction.

She called Clarky and Jessie into the lounge, where they were introduced to Grant. Jessie sat on the furthest chair and folded her arms, openly staring at Grant with a hostile face. It was the pose she liked to take when first meeting criminals in custody. Clarky was better mannered and shook Grant's hand before hovering in the doorway to the hall. Maxine was good cop, and indicated that Grant should take a seat on the sofa. It was an old, battered, two-seater leather settee and sagged in the centre from years of student use. He sat awkwardly and looked around for somewhere to rest his mug. There was a low coffee table, dappled with wine and coffee stains, so he figured that he could plant his mug there without needing to enquire whether there were any coasters.

Maxine had no choice but to sit next to him, squeezing herself as far to the side as she could so that her thigh wouldn't brush against his on the cramped, sagging sofa.

"Is this going to take long, 'cos I'm on shift tonight," Jessie said impatiently. She made a show of checking her watch.

"Oh, no, well," Grant was flustered, "it's nice to meet you all. I understand you've all been Mr Khan's tenants for a while now".

He paused and leaned forward to take his mug, but decided better of it and leant back in his seat.

"Some of us longer than others," corrected Maxine, calculating that she'd been in her front bedroom for the best part of three years now.

"You won't blame me for buying this place as an investment," Grant continued. "It can't stay in this condition, though, and it probably won't surprise you to learn that I want to do a lot of renovation work." He looked around the lounge, which remained a shrine to the 1970s. The tenants barely noticed the brown striped wallpaper, nor the orange carpet with caramel and mauve swirly patterns that looked like a child had designed it with a Spirograph. There wasn't even central heating, with just a four-bar gas fire in the lounge. Harsh winters meant hot water bottles in the bed, and wrapping up in blankets with all four bars going on the fire.

"I need to get all the plans drawn up and through the council's planning process, so that's going to take quite a few months yet. You're welcome to stay here while the works are carried out, but it's going to be disruptive, I won't lie. I plan to sell the house on once the renovations are complete. The prospect of any new owners charging you the same as Mr Khan just isn't going to happen, so I guess I'm giving you a long warning that your living arrangements are going to have to change."

It turned out that Clarky had already applied for a transfer at work and within a month scampered off to Cornwall, where he had friends and family. Jessie announced soon after that her colleague had left his wife "at last" and so Jessie planned to move in with him. That left Maxine rattling around alone in the condemned house, passing her days working for a solicitor's office, where she completed mundane tasks like filing, typing and answering the phone. It wasn't what she had envisioned when completing her university education, but there weren't many roles around for somebody with a third-class degree in sports science.

"I thought you might like to see the plans," Grant said, having turned up unannounced at the door one evening. He waggled a set of rolled-up A3 drawings at her. "I've got planning consent for the work."

It was now April and the days were longer, the trees bursting into life and Maxine was feeling more optimistic. She was pleased to see Grant, even though the rent was due, which she suspected was the primary reason for his visit.

He suggested they go for a walk, where they ended up getting merry on cider in the garden of a pub alongside the canal. The sweet smell of spring hedgerows made them heady in the warm evening sunshine. That was the start of their relationship, and Maxine never had to pay rent again. The evening walk led to proper dates, sharing beds, meeting friends, family and parents, and finally Maxine giving up her mundane job to help out with Grant's building projects. She was never acknowledged as an employee, and he only let her do tasks that couldn't be messed up, such as painting and choosing fixtures and furnishings, but by that time, his money had become a shared resource. Grant carried out the serious work with drills and sledgehammers, whilst leaving any plumbing and electrical work to contractors. Once the Exeter Terrace house was sold, they repeated the process on several other run-down properties, transforming ugly-looking, sad houses into attractive homes, and doubling Grant's investment each time.

The cottage project was an unusual diversion for Grant. He'd taken Maxine out to meet his dad for a meal in one of the villages in the vast countryside landscape between Loughborough and Grantham. Maxine had never ventured out that way before and was smitten with the traditional hamlets with thatched cottages, duckponds and village greens. The country pubs were warm and inviting, and they'd had an enjoyable evening catching up with Mr Carver Senior ("call me Don") over a Sunday roast. Like Grant, he was a property developer, and had encouraged his son to follow in his footsteps, helping out with his first projects prior to Exeter Terrace. They said their farewells and, as Grant drove Maxine out of the village, she squealed at the sight of a For Sale sign outside one of the prettiest cottages she had ever seen. She begged Grant to pull over, and they took a closer look at the whitewashed house with roses growing over the porch.

"I'll call the agent tomorrow and get the details," Grant promised. "Don't get your hopes up, though, it's probably a lot more than we can afford."

To Maxine's dismay, he was right, and it was also a lot bigger than they needed, with six bedrooms, and a garden the size of a football pitch.

"You could split it in half and create two properties," Grant's dad suggested, perusing the property's details when they next saw him. "I'll put half the money in if you need me to, and you can pay me back when you sell them off."

That had been sixteen years ago, and now as Maxine stacked the dirty plates into the dishwasher after their lasagne, she still adored the cottage as much as that first sighting. It was now a semi-detached property, with three bedrooms and a garden half the size of a football pitch, but Maxine and Grant had put their stamp on it. They'd worked their magic on the property, and sold the other half off with enough profit to pay back Grant's dad, Don.

She gazed at Grant, sitting at the island nursing his wine glass. Yes, she thought. I did bag myself the greatest catch in the East Midlands.

10

The day of the area quiz rounds came all too quickly. There had been several more trips to Jayne's house on the lead-up to the event and Mr Gray had done a marvellous job filling in gaps in their knowledge. He described places around the world that he'd travelled to, highlighting minuscule details that the children would remember. He regaled tales from history with enthusiasm and colour, and encouraged them to dress up and join in with role play. Fiona's mum was horrified to find her daughter's best t-shirt covered in tomato ketchup after having her head chopped off as Anne Boleyn to Leon's Henry the Eighth. The children gathered around and watched in fascination as Mr Gray dissected equipment around the house to demonstrate rules of physics and science. The house became a classroom by stealth.

"I'm very excited," Maxine said to Miss Earle as they took their seats in the audience. "I've brought Hector with me."

"Hector?"

"Yes, the lucky mascot. Look." Maxine wiggled the beanie toy at her teacher. She wasn't quite sure what animal it was with its four miniature, stumpy legs, and its saucer-like eyes, but it was cute, and it looked like it should be called Hector.

"He's perfect," Miss Earle agreed, smiling at Maxine encouragingly. "What makes him lucky?"

"I took him into town one afternoon and when I got home, I realised that he had fallen out of my bag," Maxine explained, hating that she was having to lie to Miss Earle. It had to be that way, though. The sisters had promised each other they would never confess the truth. "Then the amazing thing was when Trudy went to the town library the next week, she saw Hector on the shelf behind the librarian's desk. So, we think he's really lucky to have been handed in and back with us."

"That is lucky!" Miss Earle nodded.

If only she knew what really happened. The day the twins went to the library had been their introduction to devious criminality. Hector was sat on the shelf behind the librarian's desk - that part was true - but up to that point, he had never been in Maxine's possession. She spotted his doleful eyes and fell in love with him.

"Did you see that soft toy on the shelf?" she whispered to Trudy as they browsed the young adult fiction section. "It's really cute."

Trudy put the "Tale of the Wicked Witch" back in its slot and paused for thought. "I wonder if the shelf is where they keep the lost property," she replied quietly.

The thought of the toy being lost saddened Maxine. He might be destined to a life on the shelf rather than being out with an owner having adventures.

"Wait here," Trudy instructed with a stifled giggle.

Maxine watched as her sister approached the elderly lady stacking books onto a trolley near the librarian's desk.

"Excuse me, Mrs Taylor. My sister was in here last week and thinks she left her soft toy behind. Did anyone find it?"

Mrs Taylor broke out in a wide grin. "Why, yes, I think you might be in luck." She scuttled over to the shelf and seized Hector. "Is this the toy?"

Trudy clapped in delight. "Yes, it is, thank you! Maxine is going to be so pleased. She was crying herself to sleep last weekend when she found that she'd lost him."

"Well, here you go," Mrs Taylor handed him to Trudy. "Tell Maxine to be more careful with him in future."

She promised she would, and skipped back to where Maxine was observing behind the shelving.

"I can't believe you did that!" She giggled, half in awe, half in guilt. Her gain would be some other child's loss. What if the true owner really was crying him or herself to sleep over the separation? Her delight at getting hold of the toy was melting into an uncomfortable, sick feeling.

"It's not really stealing," Trudy countered. "It's more like someone else gifting it to us. If they were careless enough to lose it, then they don't deserve to have nice toys. We'll give him a great life!"

Hector did have a loving owner in Maxine from that point. She spent hours finger knitting him colourful leads and harnesses, and he accompanied her to school, to the park, and to the cinema. Hector then took the slot of lucky mascot at the quiz championships. As the team snapped up successes, Maxine became ever more convinced that Hector was truly lucky, and she made sure he was stowed in her bag on the day of her O-Levels, and then her A-Levels and even her university finals. His notoriety saved him from the culls that Maxine's mum held of other toys she had grown out of. When they were shipped off to the charity shop, trusty Hector remained in situ.

If Maxine rifled through the boxes that were about to be transported up to the new boarded-up loft, she would find Hector nestled at the bottom, underneath some dog-eared cookery books and bundle of letters from a French pen-friend that she had lost contact with years earlier.

The sisters' secret remained between them, but their parents couldn't have been cross with them, should they have discovered the devious action. There was a time, pre-Hector, that Maxine had snapped the elastic on her swimming goggles at a family trip to the pool. Once dressed, her mother marched to the reception desk of the leisure centre to ask whether a pair of goggles had been found.

The nonchalant receptionist retrieved a cardboard box from under the counter. "Everything in here has been handed in," she explained, tilting the box forward to reveal a tangled mess of goggles, hairbrushes, watches, swim trunks, and shampoo.

"Ah, that's them," her mother lied, pulling out a pair of pink Disney goggles. "There you go, Maxine. Now look after them in future." She shot a look at her baffled daughter and shooed her out of the building before she could say or do anything to spoil the con.

Back in the draughty hall of the comprehensive school hosting the local rounds of the quiz, Hector sat in Maxine's lap whilst she and Miss Earle watched proceedings unfold. There had already been several rounds held in classrooms around the site that brutally whittled the competing teams down by half with each game. Now it was time for the two semi-final rounds, held on the main school stage in front of the teachers, parents and pupils from schools that had already been knocked out. Whether it was a miracle or Hector's influence (Miss Earle thought the former whilst Maxine was convinced of the latter), Clover Bay Primary made it through to the final round, and were up against the spoilt brats of Tolchester Juniors.

They watched in awe as Jayne, Trudy, Fiona and Leon kept calm and pressed their buzzers to answer the starter questions, then sailed through the follow-up questions after a brief, sensible discussion. Just as Mr Gray had coached, Trudy was the master of the fiction questions, Leon pulled out an array of knowledge on science, history and nature, Fiona covered a lot of ground on politics and show business, whilst Jayne soaked up the gaps in their knowledge.

Tolchester Juniors put up a good fight, with a ginger spectacled boy slamming his buzzer a split second behind the Clover Bay rivals several times. The shy girl with an Alice band in her hair made several nervous mistakes, panicking as she hit the buzzer and then finding her brain had gone blank. As Clover Bay amassed points, it was clear that Tolchester Juniors were too far behind to catch up, and the hall emitted a roar of approval when the final claxon sounded.

"You were all incredible!" Miss Earle praised as they clambered back into the school minibus. "I'm so proud of you." She started the engine and fought to get first gear. "So - the next part of the competition is in

Exeter, but it's not until February, so there's plenty of time to brush up on things you were weaker on. OK?"

"Like religion," chipped in Maxine unhelpfully. "Even I know that there were three wise men that brought Jesus gifts."

"And what were the gifts?" Miss Earle challenged in reply.

Maxine blushed, and racked her brains. "Gold," she replied decisively. "And Frankenstein and …. perfume?"

Jayne started giggling at the thought of Frankenstein attending the birth of Jesus. She wasn't being cruel but Maxine felt stung.

"It's frankincense," she corrected. "Not Frankenstein."

"I have an idea," Miss Earle interjected. "We need to start writing the Nativity play for the school soon." She had recklessly volunteered to write and cast it, whilst colleague Adam had been persuaded to direct it. It had been one task too many, as now time was running short. The PTA were already aware it was planned and on her case, so she desperately needed to offload the task.

"Can I be in it, Miss?" Trudy asked.

"And me!" Fiona pleaded. "Leon will make a great Joseph. As long as Joseph blushed."

"We'll have auditions to cast it; that's only fair," Miss Earle replied firmly. "However, if you wanted to put your heads together and write the script, that would be amazing, and be a learning exercise for you."

"I like writing," Leon confirmed. "I sometimes write stories about spaceships."

The girls all looked at him in amazement and his cheeks turned crimson.

"I write stories too!" Jayne countered. "Mainly about horses and boarding schools. Hey, we could form like a writing club."

Thus, the Clover Bay writers' circle was born. It only consisted of the four members of the quiz team and Maxine, who feared she would be missing out otherwise. They met weekly at Jayne's house, which was spacious enough for them to gather around the large dining table, spreading out pens and paper, and a fat dictionary. Mrs Gray kept them topped up with orange squash and biscuits.

With the help of reference books, they researched the events surrounding the birth of Jesus and prepared a script that confirmed to Miss Earle that she'd made the right decision in getting the kids to write it. All that remained was the casting, and that's when the squabbling began.

11

"Hi Mum!" Fortuna crashed through the front door with her usual bluster. Fiona jumped. She had been miles away in thought, back at the Tolchester gymkhana in her mind. The computer hummed away in front of her, the screensaver sending starbursts over the screen whilst it patiently waited for her next keystroke.

"Oh, you're in here," Fortuna announced, entering the study and bending down to give her mum a swift kiss on the cheek. "Shall I put the kettle on?" She was already heading out towards the kitchen, not expecting an answer.

Fiona got to her feet and pulled herself together, following her daughter to the kitchen. She hovered in the doorway watching Fortuna as she swirled boiling water in the teapot to warm it. Everything was done properly in Fiona's house. Tea leaves, tea pots and proper china. The tea set had been Ted's - inherited from a great aunt years before he'd set eyes on Fiona.

Fortuna chattered on about her week at work, whilst bustling away with tea-making duties. She had inherited her chatty nature from her dad's side of the family.

"So," Fortuna finally arrived at a pause in her monologue. "What's new with you?"

"Not much," Fiona replied. It was her stock answer most weeks.

They took their seats at the country oak table and Fortuna poured milk into the tea-cups.

"Although I have had an interesting message through Facebook. It's an invite from some of the people I was at school with."

"Really?" Fortuna's interest was piqued, and she regarded her mother, wide-eyed with curiosity. "What sort of invite?" She felt a sudden protectiveness. Her mother could be drawn into all sorts of trouble with her inability to resist things. How many times had she had to nag Fiona never to click on links in emails unless she was absolutely certain it was genuine?

"I was on the school quiz team at junior school," Fiona explained. "By some sort of miracle, it turns out we were pretty good and we got all the way to the final in London where we beat the Westminster School."

"Clover Bay kids beating the private school nerds?" Fortuna gasped in disbelief.

"Yep," Fiona replied proudly. "It was in 1981, and we went to Westminster Bridge afterwards and a chap from the press team took a photograph of the four of us, which ended up in the Clover Bay Echo. I've had a message from Leon, one of the team members, asking if I would be up for recreating the photograph on the thirtieth anniversary."

Fortuna poured the tea into the cups and added a lump of sugar into her mother's.

"Leon, eh? Did you fancy him?"

"Don't be daft," Fiona protested, blushing. "He was a skinny kid that stank of farmyard. He was obsessed with spaceships and planets. But he was sweet." Judging by his profile picture, he had changed a lot, and there was a natural hesitancy in Fiona. They had all changed so much that a reunion could be a disaster. Everybody would expect things to be exactly as they used to be; carefree, easy, and harmonious.

"So, you'll say yes, right?"

"I don't know," Fiona confessed. "We'll all be so different now."

"You have to!" Fortuna countered. It would do her mother good to connect to some people outside the immediate area. "It'll only be a few hours together, so if you all hate each other at the end of it, you never have to see them again."

Fiona shrugged. "Maybe."

They sipped their tea in silence for a few minutes, before Fortuna asked who else was in the team aside from her and Leon.

"There was a girl called Trudy," she replied. "Her twin sister, Maxine, didn't make the team but used to tag along to the qualifying rounds as a lucky mascot. Their parents ran the pub close to the train station. And then the fourth member was Jayne." She didn't know where to start with a description of Jayne. She knew she would have to give her daughter an edited version of the truth, but then, that had always been the case ever since she was born. "She lived in a huge house on the cliffs, which her father had designed himself. He was an architect. God, I made such a nuisance of myself trying to be her friend because she had a horse and I was desperate to get free rides."

"I'm sure she valued your friendship," Fortuna offered generously.

"Well, I never did get many free rides," laughed Fiona in reply. She did get the horse's brushes and some free sugar, although she wasn't ready to make that confession to Fortuna yet. "The family moved away straight after the quiz final, and that's the last I ever heard of her."

There, it was the truth - that's all Fortuna needed to learn. She didn't have to mention the abrupt nature of the family's disappearance, nor the police tape strung around the property for weeks after the gang discovered that the Gray family had vanished. It would lead to more questions that Fiona didn't know the answers to.

"There will be so much catching up to do!" Fortuna enthused. "Now, what are we having for lunch?"

Their attention pulled away from Clover Bay and back into the realities of the current day, with mother and daughter enjoying a catch-up over quiche and salad before taking a stroll into town to look at the new summer collection in Marks and Spencer.

It was only after Fortuna departed on the train back to London that Fiona allowed herself to sit quietly in the lounge and transport herself back to the summer of 1981.

She couldn't quite recall what she had been watching that Saturday morning on TV, but she remembered the trill of the phone ringing in the kitchen and Darryl answering.

"It's Trudy," he grunted, clearly disappointed that the call wasn't for him.

Fiona grabbed the receiver from him and shooed him away. It was a needless act. He had no intention of hanging around to listen to the conversation of his younger sibling.

"Something is happening up at Jayne's house," Trudy gabbled breathlessly without any pre-amble. "Maxine and I are going up to check it out."

"What do you mean, 'something's happening'?"

"Don't know, that's why we've got to check it out. Meet us at the cockle hut in twenty minutes. I'll call Leon."

Fiona stared at the receiver that was left abruptly broadcasting the silence of a terminated conversation. Trudy explained more as the friends gathered on the seafront twenty minutes later. One of the customers in her parents' pub had come in saying that the police were crawling all over "that fancy place on the west cliff" but he didn't know what it was all about.

"Maybe they've been burgled," Leon speculated on the walk up the lane. "I bet Mrs Gray has got some expensive jewellery. We might be able to help find the thief!"

"You've been watching too much Hart to Hart," chuckled Maxine.

They were sobered by the sight of a police van parked on the lane, and, beyond that, police tape lined the boundary of the property. There was no sign of the horses grazing in the paddock to the side of the house. Fiona noticed that the horsebox and Land Rover were also missing. Several more police cars littered the lane, and they could see men in their black uniforms moving around the gardens. A portly policeman guarded the gate as the foursome approached hesitantly.

"Nothing to see here, kids," he confirmed as they hovered at the gate.

"Move along."

"We've come to call on our friend, Jayne," Trudy retorted. "She lives here," she added needlessly.

All four tried to peer around the bulk of the policeman to see what was happening at the house.

"Sorry kids, there's nobody home."

"Do you know when they'll be back?"

"I've got no information," he replied firmly.

The four children dithered on the pavement, mulling over their options, which seemed limited.

"Come on," sighed Leon at last, "let's go. We can always come back tomorrow."

Fiona couldn't remember whether they did go back the next day, but there was never anything in the Clover Bay Echo about the disappearance, and after a couple of days even the customers in the Five Bells stopped gossiping and speculating. Fiona recalled going back to the house once the police had retreated from the property, taking their vans and protective tape with them. All that remained was the empty property, standing silent, with the waves crashing into the cliffs behind it.

Fiona jolted herself back to 2011, padded back into her study and re-read Leon's message once more. She copied his email address into a new email and began to type her response.

12

Jayne took the lead in writing the script for the Christmas Nativity. Gathered around the large family dining table, the objective of the inaugural session was to define the characters needed for the play. Miss Earle had given them a few pointers, and Mr Crump, the portly music teacher, had outlined the hymns they'd need to include.

Jayne sat with her fountain pen poised above the blank page, waiting for the others to contribute. Sometimes she felt like she was having to do everything herself.

"So we need a narrator," she prompted.

"Really?" queried Trudy. "Why?"

"To explain to the audience what's going on."

"But that's daft!" Leon argued. "You don't have a narrator in Emmerdale Farm. The characters speak and that's how the audience know what's going on."

"You need a donkey," interjected Fiona. "Do you think we could use your horse as a donkey, Jayne?"

"Hang on, hang on," Jayne held up her hands, frustrated. "A donkey isn't a character and I don't think the school will allow live animals in the hall."

"They might, and the donkey is a character. Mary has to ride the donkey to the inn, so it's an important role in the play." Leon pointed out.

Jayne shrugged. "Let's ask Miss Earle."

"I want to play Mary," Fiona stated. "Do you think we could get a real baby?"

"I think I'd rather play a wise man than Joseph," Leon mused. "At least I won't have to kiss anyone."

"Urgh!" Maxine recoiled. "Does Joseph have to kiss Mary then?"

"Let's focus," Jayne ordered. The foursome fell silent. "So, we have a narrator, and Mary, and Joseph…."

She stopped writing and looked up, giving them a chance to contribute.

"The donkey?" Fiona prompted.

"The baby Jesus," Maxine offered, proud to have been helpful.

Wordlessly, Jayne wrote them down.

"The innkeeper," Trudy said. "Like my dad!"

"Three wise men," Leon said. "Oh, and weren't there some sheep? My dad can get us real sheep if we need some. He's a dairy farmer so he has loads of cows but he knows Mr Evans up the lane who has sheep."

"We'll ask Miss Earle," Jayne replied with a resigned sigh. "And what comes with sheep?"

"A sheepdog!" Maxine declared triumphantly.

"A shepherd," Trudy corrected her, rolling her eyes in despair. "What about an angel? Wasn't there an angel?"

"Do we really need three wise men?" Leon queried. "I know the Bible said there were three, but if we haven't got enough lines for all three wise men, then it's not really fair."

"Yes, we'll have three, and they will all have some lines," Jayne replied, unable to keep the exasperation out of her voice.

The five friends managed to get a cast of characters concluded within an hour, and Jayne conceded that they could play some games to celebrate. She suggested hide and seek, as the game provided her with a few minutes' peace. A break from inane comments from Maxine and pointless questions from Leon and Fiona digressing about babies and donkeys. She liked her school friends, but they could be wearing.

"Can we hide anywhere?" Fiona asked, already plotting where she would go.

"Anywhere except Nina's room," Jayne confirmed. She would start by seeking, she asserted, as she knew all the rooms. As Jayne began counting to thirty, the friends scampered off. Leon shot down to the basement, an area that fascinated him with the toys and games available. Trudy and Maxine trotted up the stairs, and both burst into Jayne's bedroom.

"We can't both be in here," Maxine whined, but Trudy ignored her and shimmied underneath the bed. Maxine had already planned to hide in Jayne's vast closet, so opened up the louvred doors and nestled into a pile of sweaters in the corner, and quietly pulled the door shut behind her. It fell dark, with shafts of light falling through the slats.

They stayed silent as they heard Jayne call that ready or not, she was coming. The minutes passed by and there was no sound but the ticking of the alarm clock on Jayne's bedside table. Jayne was in no hurry to seek the gang. She would relish the peace and quiet too. She checked the downstairs first, finding an empty downstairs toilet, and nobody in the cupboard under the stairs. She wandered into the lounge and thumped the cushions, even though she knew there was no room for any of them to have successfully hidden under them. She opened the doors of the kitchen cupboards, again, knowing that the spaces were too small to fit a ten-year-old, but it was all part of being systematic.

Upstairs, Maxine was finding boredom setting in. She glanced around the dim exterior of the closet and discovered a wooden box balancing on the top of a pile of books on the floor in the opposite corner. Out of curiosity she reached out and quietly brought the box to her lap. She eased off the lid and found a treasure trove of jewellery nestled inside. She picked her way through the contents. In a little white cardboard box sat a gold ring with the letter "J" embossed on the surface. She tested its size against her fingers but it would only fit her little pinkie. She replaced that and found a gold bracelet adorned with sparkly diamonds. They could have been real or fake; Maxine couldn't tell, but it was a gorgeous bracelet.

"Somebody must be up here," Jayne's voice floated through the upper floor, making Maxine jump. The box fell from the precariously balanced spot on her knees, spewing the contents around the shadows of the floor. Oh goodness, Maxine panicked. She scrabbled around her feet, scooping up the contents of the box and cramming it all back into place. The lid went back on and she placed the box back onto the top of the books, just in time.

"Found you!" She heard Trudy groan as her hiding place under the bed was rumbled. "You lose, and have to be "it" next."

"Am I the first then?" Trudy grumbled from the other side of the closet door.

Maxine knew that it would only be a matter of time before her protection was pulled back to reveal her hiding spot. She'd have to try harder next time. A glimmer from the floor caught her attention and with horror, she realised it was a stray piece of jewellery that she'd failed to replace. She grabbed at it and only had time to note it was a piece of chunky glass with a black chain that reminded her of liquorice. As she sensed Jayne's presence outside the closet, she thrust the necklace deep into her cardigan pocket. She could always hide in the same place next time, and put it back properly.

"Found you!" Jayne announced, pulling back the louvred door to reveal Maxine.

The sisters traipsed around after Jayne as she checked her parents' bedroom and bathroom, finding neither Leon nor Fiona.

"I bet Leon's in the basement," Jayne concluded, galloping down to the hall, and heading for the wooden staircase to the lower floor. They heard the sound of the pinball machine before they saw Leon completely engrossed in his game. The lure of the free pinball machine had over ridden his desire to hide.

"I bet no-one can beat my score!" boasted Leon, as he flicked the buttons with an aggressiveness the girls weren't used to seeing.

"I bet I can," Trudy rose to the challenge, and suddenly the friends were completely distracted from the game of hide and seek altogether. As

Maxine watched Trudy start her assault on Leon's score, she slid her hand into her cardigan pocket and felt her fingers run across the necklace. A guilty flush of shame ran through her. She really needed to put it back.

"Shall we do the next round of hide and seek?" Maxine asked, trying to get her plan back on track.

"Oh!" Jayne suddenly gasped. "We haven't found Fiona yet."

"Let me finish this game first…" Trudy protested.

"Come on Max, let's go and look for Fiona," Jayne said, making her way back towards the stairs. "We'll leave those two battling it out for pinball glory."

And so, the repatriation of the necklace failed. Fiona's sneaky decision to go outside and hide in the tack room was genius, as it took Jayne and Maxine another fifteen minutes of hunting every inch of the house, and then the garden, to find her. Like Leon, she was distracted by the treasures she had discovered in the dusty outbuilding to be bothered to hide properly, and they eventually found her inspecting the parts of the bridle that belonged to Beauty.

It took another quarter of an hour to extract Fiona from the treasure trove, as she bombarded Jayne with questions about what the various pieces of tack did, how was it cleaned, what function did each brush have?

By the time the trio made their way back to the house, Mrs Gray met them with the news that it was time for them all to go home, as the Gray family had a diary date with Jayne's parents' friends in Tolchester.

Maxine and Trudy waved goodbye to Leon, and he and his red Chopper bike sped down the hill and out of sight. The twins walked back home together, Maxine's hand remaining in her pocket, turning the glass block of the necklace over and over in her fingertips. She decided not to tell her sister about the inadvertent stealing of Jayne's jewellery and felt it was too risky to try and get it back into Jayne's wardrobe in the future. No, she decided. She would hide it away and never tell anyone about it.

Even now, if Maxine were to rummage around in some of the boxes destined for the loft in her cottage in 2011, she would discover her childhood jewellery box. There, in the delicate bottom drawer beneath the rotating ballerina, was still the Murano glass necklace wrapped in tissue paper that hadn't seen the light of day for thirty years.

13

Leon was exhausted. He'd had a couple of meetings with new suppliers, interviewed a string of school leavers for waitressing roles in the café, had to referee an altercation in the car park when a pensioner reversed into a parked motorcycle, fought with the printer when it insisted the ink was low, and had to serve on the butchery counter for a couple of hours when Jake rang in sick.

"It never stops," he moaned to Sasha, finally sinking into the battered armchair after cashing up and taking the thirty second commute on foot to their home around the corner from the farm shop. Naturally, his house was one of the farm's old barns, tastefully converted to give separation from his parents who still occupied the farmhouse of his childhood.

Sasha stopped chopping vegetables and flicked on the kettle. A cup of tea before supper would soothe him.

"Thanks, love," he sighed as she placed it down on the occasional table at his side. He smiled up at her, grateful that she'd come into his life five years ago, complete with her purple hair, vegan principles and a rescued greyhound called Droopy. She had been wanting to help with the harvest, having rambled on foot along the south coast footpath, wandering to wherever a spot of work could fund the next stage of her travels.

"It's July," Leon had replied with a baffled furrow of his forehead. "There's nothing to harvest until September."

Her face fell and an awkward silence lingered between them. Sasha wasn't ready to continue hiking westwards. Droopy dropped to the ground and rested his head on his front paws in weary resignation.

"I do have some odd jobs you could do, though, if you don't mind getting your hands dirty," Leon offered. The more he thought about the mountain of tasks that he never seemed to get around to tackling, the more appealing Sasha's arrival was. She pitched a battered tent on a shady spot at the edge of the orchard, and worked her way through Leon's list of tasks, from weeding his parents' garden and painting the fence in the car park to clearing out a disused outbuilding. There was nothing she wouldn't turn her hand to. Within weeks she became indispensable to him. Within a few more weeks they became lovers and here they were, five years down the road, contentedly sharing out the tasks around the business. Except the butcher's counter, of course, which vegan Sasha refused to entertain.

"You've had an email from that Fiona," she pointed out. Leon had explained about the twins' visit and their mission to reunite the quiz team for the photograph in London.

Leon's heart beat quicker. Like Maxine, he'd been sceptical that the Fiona Farr of 1981 would grow up to have a double-barrelled surname, and wasn't expecting to have contacted the correct person.

"What did she say?" Leon reached for his laptop, where both he and Sasha shared an email account.

"Read it for yourself," Sasha replied with a grin.

Leon clicked open the email programme and saw, nestled in the inbox between an invoice from a supplier and a newsletter from The British Science Fiction Association, a sender called Fiona Foxham-Farr.

"Dear Leon," he read. "It was a lovely, unexpected surprise to get a message from you."

"Wow," he remarked to Sasha, who was still observing him with that enigmatic grin of hers. "We found the right one!"

He turned his attention back to the email, which he could see, was going to be a lengthy read. "I haven't had any contact with anyone from Clover Bay for a couple of decades now, and it was great that you reached out. I hope you and Maxine and Trudy are all well. I'd love to hear all your news.

As you may remember, I moved away from Clover Bay in 1986 when my mum met a new man, and he persuaded her to uproot and start a new life in London. We'd just finished our O-Levels, and the thought of London was far more exciting than staying in Clover Bay.

I went to college in London and got a couple of A-Levels under my belt, before securing a job in an estate agency, Foxhams. Typical of me, I go and fall in love with my boss and the owner of the chain of estate agents, Ted, and we married in 1991 and had a daughter, Fortuna."

Leon paused, amused. It was no surprise that Fiona had had a child at the tender age of twenty-one, but he couldn't reconcile the Fiona he knew with calling a daughter Fortuna. Kylie, maybe, or Brittany or Amanda. Those names were a possibility, but not the pretentiousness of naming a baby after a goddess of fortune. He shrugged. People were full of surprises.

"Sadly, I lost my darling Ted in 2007," he read on, "and Fortuna lives in London now where she works for the family business. So, I'm left here rattling around a cottage in Kent, trying to keep myself busy. I volunteer for a local animal rescue charity and spend an obscene amount of time in the garden".

60

Leon longed to see what Fiona looked like these days. She sounded more middle aged than his parents!

Fiona's attention turned to Leon and the twins, asking after them, their families and what they were up to. She asked whether they had tracked down Jayne.

"I'd love to know what happened to Jayne," she ended her email. "I have fond memories of spending time at her place, practising quiz questions, playing hide and seek, and that amazing games room in the basement. Most of all, I'd like to know why the family disappeared so suddenly. If you haven't found her, how do you propose we do? I looked on Facebook, but there are too many Jayne Grays... and that's probably not her name any longer."

She had signed off abruptly, leaving a contact number if they wanted to call her.

He looked up at Sasha. "How the hell are we going to find Jayne?" he mused out loud.

14

"Are you awake, Jayne?" Fiona's urgent hiss came down from the creaking bunk above.

Of course, I'm awake, thought Jayne. The mattress was strange, the sheets felt crumpled and smelled of a stale odour that she couldn't place. There were constant noises drifting into the dark bedroom from outside that made Jayne fear the worst. Car doors slamming could be gangs breaking the door down, angry shouts could escalate into violence, and a distant dog was barking relentlessly. She missed the familiar sounds of home. She was used to the soothing sound of the sea at night - the waves slapping rhythmically against the rocks from a safe distance at the end of the property, the occasional neigh from the stable and the hypnotic tick of the grandfather clock on the landing.

She had agreed to sleep over at Fiona's out of politeness. She hadn't wanted to, but had no excuse to hand when Fiona invited her. "It doesn't seem fair that we're always round here," Fiona had explained in the hallway of the Grays' house as she tugged on her dirty pumps in readiness to go home. "So, my mum says it's OK for you to come over for tea and stay at mine on Friday. Daryll's away on a school trip so you can have his bed."

Mrs Gray was hovering in the doorway and chipped in before any response had formed on Jayne's lips. "That's really kind, Fiona. Please thank your mum. Jayne will be delighted to come."

"Do I really have to go?" Jayne protested once Fiona had left the house, but Mrs Gray thought it would do Jayne good to get out and see how other people lived. She was acutely aware that not everyone shared the privilege that they did, and to go and share the hospitality of the girl whose clothes were always dirty, usually ill-fitting and who always appreciated taking leftovers home, would instil some humility into Jayne.

When Mrs Gray pulled the Range Rover up outside Fiona's squat, terraced house, she was determined not to betray her principals, and forced a smile onto her face.

The house looked sad and neglected, its dirty cream exterior was weather beaten and forlorn.

"You don't have to walk me right to the door," Jayne scolded moodily as her mother shook off the seatbelt and made to open her driver's door. If her friends could negotiate Clover Bay on their bikes, roller skates and on foot, she could at least make it up the garden path alone.

"Well, give me a kiss then," Mrs Gray negotiated, offering up her cheek. "I'll stay and make sure you get in OK."

As Jayne rolled her eyes and pecked her mother on the cheek, a wave of Yves Saint Laurent drifted up her nostrils. She didn't know it yet, but it would be the last pleasant smell she encountered for a while.

She retrieved her duffel bag from the back seat and waded through a sea of knee-high dandelions that had sprawled their way over the path from the unkempt front garden.

The door opened before Jayne had reached for the rusty door knocker.

"Hi Jayne. Come in!" Fiona was bursting with excitement and held the door wide for Jayne to step through into the gloomy passageway. The stale smell of Fiona's mum's 20-a-day habit assaulted her nostrils.

"Shall I take my shoes off?" Jayne asked. She had been taught that it was always polite to ask when visiting other people's homes.

"God, no," laughed Fiona. "You'd probably hurt yourself on a nail or something before we got to the stairs. Let me give you a tour. It won't take long though, as our house is quite small."

She led the way into the lounge that came off the hallway to the right. It looked like a patchwork of unfinished DIY projects to Jayne, with wallpaper applied by an amateur on one wall and pink paint on the other wall, whilst the bare floorboards had been sanded down and then abandoned.

"Have you lived here long?" Jayne asked, wondering whether the refurbishment was in the pipeline. She scanned the room. Above the dusty stones of the fireplace hung a framed print of frolicking puppies. Although it brightened the walls, Jayne wondered who had purchased the picture and hung it with pride. It was presumably a find in a jumble sale, cheap market or a charity shop, and held no personal connection to the Farr family.

"I've lived here all my life," Fiona replied. "The council should have let my mum move to a bigger house when I was born, but they keep telling her there aren't any available. Mum says it will become more urgent when I get older, as a teenage girl should have privacy from an elder brother." The words were straight out of Fiona's mother's mouth.

They moved through to the cramped galley kitchen, overflowing with belongings on the counter tops. Jayne scanned the discarded carrier bags, loose coins, empty cigarette packets, unopened mail, ashtrays (full, of course) and what looked like a scattering of cat biscuits. The orange lino was cracked and felt tacky underfoot. Jayne was glad she had kept her shoes on.

"Come and see my bedroom," Fiona urged, leading the way up the stairs. The room at the back had a large window overlooking the scruffy rear garden, where weeds had won the battle against the grass. Bunk beds dominated one side of the room, and the walls displayed posters of topless women that Daryll had cut from the tabloid newspapers. Apart from a battered chest spewing fabrics from its broken drawers, there were no other possessions. Jayne wondered what they were going to play with.

"Is your mum home?" Jayne asked, realising how quiet the house was.

"No, she's been at work and is going out with her friend, Alison, afterwards. She calls it Malibu Friday. She's left a pizza for us to have."

Jayne's mum would have been horrified to see her daughter tucking into a cheap pepperoni pizza and fizzy pop for tea. Jayne, on the other hand, was impressed to see how Fiona navigated the grill and managed to warm the pizza with only a couple of areas of the crust that blackened. The strawberry flavoured fizzy pop tasted manufactured and falsely sweet, but it made a change to Jayne's regular Friday night diet.

"So, what do you want to do now?" Fiona asked, stacking their crumb laden plates into the sink.

Jayne glanced blankly around the kitchen, hunting for inspiration. "Er… what would you normally do?"

"Watch a bit of telly. Dallas is on Friday nights, but's it's not on yet. Or we could go and light a fire behind next door's shed. There's a kind of den behind there and we sometimes light bits of dried grass. It's a bit boring, though. Or we can put on Daryll's cassettes and dance."

None of it sounded appealing to Jayne, who shrugged politely. "I don't mind. Whatever you prefer."

Fiona led the way back through to the lounge and crouched down in front of a bookshelf where, amongst the mess of papers and empty cigarette boxes, she pulled out a shoebox that harboured a stack of cassette tapes.

"Daryll nicks them from Woolworths," she explained, sliding one into the gaping jaws of a battered tape player on the middle shelf. "Do you like The Specials?"

A powerful beat started up from the player and Fiona turned the volume switch to fill the lounge with ska.

"I've not heard of them," she admitted.

"What music do you like, then? I can ask Daryll to nick you a cassette next time he's in town."

Fiona had started to bounce to the beat as Jayne looked on self-consciously.

"Um, I like Simon and Garfunkel. And Abba. Daryll doesn't have to steal me a cassette, though. My dad has most of their albums."

"You've done too much, much too young," Fiona sang happily. Her arms flapped at her side like a drunk seagull. "Now you're married with a kid, when you could be having fun with meeeee."

Jayne's foot began to tap and as the song's refrain repeated, she felt herself loosen up and managed to step from side to side.

"That's it. Go wild!" Fiona encouraged.

When the cassette got to its half way point and Fiona flipped it over, Jayne had started to get the hang of dancing to ska, and would almost admit to enjoying herself. But once in bed, she was counting down the hours until she could escape home again. She didn't realise that things were about to get worse, but as Fiona's voice came down from the top bunk, she wondered what Fiona wanted. The illuminated numbers on the clock radio said 02:32.

"Yes, I'm awake," she whispered back.

The lump above her shifted and thumped down to the floor. "Great. Get dressed. We're going on an adventure."

In the darkness she could sense Fiona pulling on her jeans.

"What? Where?" Jayne replied in panic.

"It's a surprise."

Jayne didn't like surprises. Her pink pedal pushers were thrust at her, with the repeated instruction to get dressed.

Reluctantly she eased out of her bunk and pulled them on under her nightie.

"Just pull your coat over your night dress," Fiona ordered.

"I didn't bring a coat."

Fiona rifled into the drawers and pulled out a stained shell suit jacket. "There you go - it's Daryll's so it's probably too big, but it'll do."

Fiona opened the bedroom door and peered over the landing to make sure the coast was clear. She'd heard her mother arrive home and go to bed a while ago, and there was no light coming from under her mum's bedroom door.

"Make sure you only step on the stairs that I step on, as I know which ones will creak, so I avoid them."

Obediently Jayne tiptoed after Fiona's shadow and, as her eyes adjusted to the darkness, was able to navigate to the front door without accidentally stepping on a creaking stair.

"Wait here. I just need to get a knife for protection," Fiona added, hurrying quickly to the kitchen, leaving Jayne open-mouthed in the hallway. She pulled a paring knife from a wonky drawer and stowed it in her front coat pocket.

She put the front door on the latch, and stepped out into the garden. Jayne followed, her heart pounding with the fear of the unknown. The air was crisp and cool, and a fat moon glowed down on them. The stillness was seductive. In the distance, a cat yowled its territorial warning to another.

"Isn't this amazing?" Fiona asked rhetorically. "I do this a lot. It's kind of liberating."

Their footsteps sounded loud slapping on the pavement as the girls headed further into the estate.

"Where are we going?" Jayne repeated, looking over her shoulder every few seconds.

"Across town," Fiona replied enigmatically. "You'll see."

Jayne wished she'd worn her boots. Her dainty pink ballet shoes were no match for the wintery bite of the wind, and she could feel her toes going numb.

Fiona led them down a graffiti strewn alleyway that Jayne would avoid in daylight hours, let alone in the pitch-black of night. Fiona strode on, pausing only to point out a fox that was snuffling in a bin near the bus stop.

The pair emerged on the main Tolchester Road and Jayne recognised where they were. She hoped Fiona would loop back towards her estate, but she continued to head towards the seafront.

"Know where we are?" she grinned, pausing outside a wooden gate that led into a beer garden. Jayne looked at the pub. Its sign depicting Five Bells was creaking in the breeze on its rusty hooks. She shook her head.

"It's where Maxine and Trudy live. Come on." Without waiting for a response, Fiona pushed the wooden gate open and circumnavigated the garden on the grass. With a roll of her eyes, Jayne followed. Across the far side of the garden, through a thicket of trees, was a stone outbuilding. Incredulously the door was unlocked and Fiona pulled it open wide and motioned for Jayne to enter. Inside, shelves were stacked neatly with all the stock for the pub.

"Wow," Jayne gasped. "This is bigger than my mum's store cupboard!" She looked around the gloom, which was being illuminated by a streetlight on the other side of the pub's boundary wall. Her eyes scanned over the catering packs of baked beans, tinned peaches, cans of pop and packs of peanuts attached to cardboard displays. She'd never seen so many boxes of crisps piled up before.

Fiona was tugging at the plastic wrapping on a 12-pack of Coke cans. "There you go," she said, liberating one of the cans and holding it out towards Jayne. She eyed it suspiciously. Her mother forbade her to drink fizzy drinks, but it was the theft that troubled her more deeply.

"We can't just help ourselves," Jayne scolded. "That's stealing."

Fiona shrugged and opened the can for herself, taking an appreciative swig and burping contentedly. "They're our friends. It's not stealing if it's from your friends."

Jayne couldn't see the logic but didn't have the energy to argue. "Can we go soon?" she pleaded. "It's very late."

"Yeah, in a minute," Fiona replied dismissively. She gulped down the rest of the Coke and scrunched up the can, stuffing it behind a box in the corner where she figured it wouldn't be discovered for a while. She pondered the stack of crisp boxes, unable to decide between Cheese and Onion and Monster Munch. In the end she opened both boxes and took a packet of each for the journey home.

"Come on then," she conceded, reluctantly heading for the door. She'd wanted to stay for hours. She thought Jayne would have loved sharing the secret space with her, enjoying the hospitality and the cherishing a small rebellion.

It looked like she'd misjudged the situation, and that wasn't helping her mission to become best buddies with Jayne. She vowed to try harder.

15

The writers' circle met after school on the first Tuesday of each month, with the first one taking place in December. The Nativity script was already signed off, and Mr Crump had composed some songs to complement the story. After a biased audition process, Miss Earle had cast the roles with Mr Crump's blessing.

As a reward for doing the lion's share of the script writing, the quiz team were rewarded with the best roles. Jayne secured the plum part of the narrator, which held the most lines, and meant she wouldn't have to wear a daft costume. She would be allowed to put on a smart dress and look grown up. She may even be allowed to wear some make-up, which her mother normally forbade.

Trudy was cast as Mary, with the cheeky charm of Jason Waterford as Joseph. Neither realised at the time that they would be swapping the swaddled doll for a real-life baby of their own just seven years later.

Leon, as farmer's son, was cast as the lead shepherd, but any living, breathing livestock was banned by Miss Earle. Fiona became the angel, complete with a makeshift tinfoil halo and wings resplendent with tinsel that had been rescued from a school cupboard full of scrap materials. Maxine, the weakest actor of the pack, had initially been pencilled in as third shepherd, but she managed to argue that as she lived in a pub, she had the experience to play the part of the innkeeper.

Their lives became consumed with rehearsals for the Nativity, practice for the quiz, and now the added calendar date of the writers' circle.

"What do we even do at a writers' circle?" Maxine asked as they were all installed around the Grays' dining table once again. She didn't want to be there, but the prospect of being left out was worse.

"We write stuff," replied Leon unhelpfully. Jayne had laid out sheets of lined A4 paper at every place setting and piled a heap of ballpoint pens in the centre of the table.

"We'll take a theme, and then have an hour to all write something on that topic, then we'll read our work out to each other and comment."

"So, what's the theme?" Fiona asked. "Could we write about ponies?"

"I was thinking we could write about aliens... or science fiction in general," replied Jayne, who had already given the evening's proceedings a lot of thought, and had a story formed in her head.

"Why don't we just write whatever we want?" Trudy suggested. She knew Maxine would struggle to formulate any story about outer space.

"Ok," Jayne conceded. The last thing she wanted as to waste a lot of precious time arguing. "Let's write until eight o'clock, and then we'll share what we've written."

She immediately began to construct her story, her head bent conscientiously over the page. Leon took a pen and began to write a sentence before striking it through and starting again.

Trudy had also been giving her masterpiece some thought. Inspired by rehearsals with Jason, she was going to draft a story of romance, where the mousey girl was in love with the charming boy from the village, and then, to her surprise, he told her that he was in love with her.

Maxine sucked on the top of the pen. She loved that there was a hole in the top of the pen lid and it gave a whistle when she sucked in on it.

"Cut it out," her sister scolded.

Maxine sighed. She figured she could try to write a poem about running, but struggled to think of a word to rhyme with running. She glanced around the table. Jayne was scribbling furiously and had filled up half of her first page already, whilst Leon had managed a couple of paragraphs, scarred with multiple strikethroughs where he changed his mind. Fiona was sketching a horse, although its proportions were misjudged and its eyelashes were as long as its mane. Trudy wrote slowly and methodically, a contented smile on her lips as she pictured a scene in which the poor girl with the plain clothes had struck up a conversation with the handsome boy in the village.

"I like to run," wrote Maxine, desperate to get something on the page. "It's a lot of fun." Ha! This poetry thing was easy after all. "It's nice in the sun. Everyone should run."

There. She was finished.

"Are we all done?" Jayne asked when the hour was up.

"I'm struggling a bit," confessed Leon, looking down at his messy page with shame. "But I thought I could work on it at home and bring it back next time."

"Yeah, me too." Trudy jumped on his good idea.

"Oh, OK." Jayne was taken aback. How could they not have produced a finished story within an hour?

"I've finished," Maxine interjected proudly. "I've written a short poem about running."

The foursome gave a polite ripple of applause at the end of Maxine's four simple lines, and she beamed with pride.

"I'm not very good at writing but I've drawn a horse." Fiona held up her picture. "I don't think I've got the tack right, but maybe you could show me some time?" she asked of Jayne. "Now your turn. Let's hear your story."

"Very well," Jayne conceded. She picked up her piece of paper and glanced around the table to check she had everyone's full attention. "It's called 'The Book Club'. By Jayne Gray." She cleared her throat and began to read. "The book club had not got off to a good start. Simeon and Nigel had never met before and now they were sitting in an alcove in The Dog and Duck waiting to see whether more people would turn up.

The advertised start time was five minutes ago and Nigel had drunk too much beer and now needed the toilet. He decided to try and take his mind off it.

'What's the book about?' he asked Simeon, nodding at the paperback on the table in front of him.

Simeon looked up at him and sighed. 'Shouldn't we wait for any others first?'

'I think we may be the lot,' said Nigel. 'We may as well start.'

Simeon looked directly at him. 'It's my own book actually. It's a true story that I wrote about me, and about a long journey that I made across space.'"

Leon perked up when he realised that Jayne had written a sci-fi story. He put down his pen and listened carefully.

Jayne read on. "'You see, there is alien life in the universe. People don't think that there is, but there is, and I've seen it for myself. Let me tell you, Nigel, that discovering other species in the galaxy has not been a positive experience. You see, I was a space traveller and I was offered the chance to take part in a secret mission to try and contact extra-terrestrial life. It was a top-secret mission, and one that I have had to live with for years. But I needed to tell my story, so I wrote this book. I can't live with it any longer.'

Nigel looked both intrigued, and a little sceptical. 'Tell me more,' he said.

Simeon continued. 'I travelled alone, in my spacecraft, and I actually landed on a planet on which there was alien life. The people there looked like me but that is where the similarity ended. The inhabitants were cruel, ignorant and spiteful. They stole from each other and gloated about how much they had. Those who had less were treated with distaste and cast aside. They had a beautiful planet but seemed intent on abusing it. It was horrible. And that wasn't the worst bit, Nigel. Not by a long shot. When I could take it no more, I returned to my spaceship and it wouldn't work. It wouldn't start and there was absolutely nothing I could do.'

'My god, that's awful,' said Nigel. 'How did you manage to get back?'

Simeon raised his head and couldn't stop the tears pricking at his eyes. 'I didn't,' he whispered, so quietly that Nigel struggled to hear him. 'I'm still here.' The end."

There was stunned silence from the friends around the table.

"That's amazing!" Leon enthused. "I could never think up a twist like that."

Jayne shrugged modestly. "It needs a bit of polishing."

"You should enter it into a competition or something," Leon persisted.

"I don't get it," Maxine whined, but the rest of the gang ignored her. Jayne pushed the sheaves of paper to one side and rose from the table to stretch. Remembering that she was still the hostess, she took drinks requests from them and bustled off to the kitchen to fetch them.

Leon picked up his yellow plastic ADIDAS bag from the floor and carefully stowed his scribble strewn sheets into the bag. He was disheartened to discover that he would never write as fluidly and concisely as Jayne, whose manuscript lay just within reach. Temptation gnawed at him. He glanced around the table where Max and Trudy were absorbed in a game trying to stab each other's hands with felt tip pens. Fiona had left the table to go to the bathroom. Before he could change his mind, he grabbed at Jayne's story and slid the pages into his bag. If challenged, it would look like an innocent accident.

Jayne's attention was far from the story, though, and, on returning to the table, she invited them to go to the den to see the new video cassette recorder that Mr Gray had brought home that afternoon.

The inaugural meeting of the writers' circle was finished, but for Leon it was the start of a deception that he would feel guilty about for many years to come.

16

The plan to track down Jayne was weak and unstructured. Beyond using internet search engines to query the names of the Gray family, the foursome struggled. Maxine had heard about a website that put family trees together, and could draw on census data and other official records to track down where the family could have moved to after their disappearance in 1981. She signed up for a 30-day free trial and tried to navigate around the software, but without knowing where any of them were born nor their exact dates of birth, the plan quickly failed.

Trudy wondered whether the key to tracking the family down might be to discover what happened at the house. She tried to get hold of local newspaper archives from 1981, but the online records stopped at 1995, and she was told that the earlier editions were all on microfiche in the library. Trawling through page by page could prove to be a fruitless task and, exhausted by the mere idea of it, Trudy wasn't willing to offer up her precious time to do that.

Fiona had a friend in the village whose daughter worked in the police, and she asked her how easy it would be to look up police records. Anything was worth a try, she figured.

"Looking it up would be easy," her friend relayed to her after she had consulted her daughter. "But losing her job would be less palatable."

They all tried asking their parents if they had any recollection of the time. Leon's parents claimed that they knew nothing about his school friends from that long ago; they were far too busy. The twins called their parents in the Spanish sunshine and, whilst their mum had a vague recollection of a scandal being discussed in the pub, the details evaded her.

Fiona's mum would have been the most knowledgeable on the subject. Being a social worker (which Mr and Mrs Gray found most ironic) led her to learn all sorts of secrets about the families of Clover Bay during her time there. Unfortunately, the years of smoking had taken its toll on her health, and she'd passed away from lung cancer in 2008, taking her insight with her.

By comparison, the hunt for Miss Earle had been uncomplicated. The headteacher of Clover Bay Primary, Mr Riley, had stayed in touch with

Susie Earle since their days as young, fresh-faced teachers. Although she had left Clover Bay Primary School in the mid-eighties and moved up to London, she had regularly written to Mr Riley to keep in touch. Paper letters turned to electronic communications over the years, except for the annual Christmas cards that she sent without fail.

She emailed back to him with the positive news that she would be happy to be part of the photo in June, and gave her permission for her email address to be passed on to members of the quiz team. Whilst she couldn't quite recall what they all looked like in 1981, she remembered the group, and their quiz prowess, and was fascinated to learn what they had all grown up to be. She vaguely recalled asking them what they wanted to be when they grew up. It was on the train ride back to Clover Bay from London on that balmy afternoon in 1981. They were all giddy with success, and, unbeknownst to the youngsters, Susie Earle was buzzing from building bridges with her ex. The conversation had turned when Jayne asked Miss Earle why she had become a teacher. She gave some predictable answer about wanting to help children develop, and asked the same question back to the quiz champions.

"I want to be a vet," Fiona announced decisively. "I want to make animals feel better."

"You have to put them to sleep too," Jayne was quick to point out. "Nina's pony Spangle was put down when he got colic last year. She cried loads."

"I want to work with books," Trudy offered. "Maybe something like a librarian. Or have my own bookshop. I love the little bookshop down in Hope Square. Mrs Trueman gives us sweets when we go in, even if we don't buy a book."

"Well, I want to write books. I think it would be cool to be the biggest selling science fiction author on the planet," gushed Leon. "It would be amazing for everyone to know your name, but not necessarily know what you look like, so you wouldn't get bothered like pop stars are. But I'd still be very rich."

"What about you, Maxine?" Miss Earle asked, noticing that Maxine was quietly staring out at the blur of green passing the train window.

"I don't know yet," she sighed. "I'm not clever enough to be a vet or a writer."

"Maybe you'll be representing Great Britain at the Olympics in a few years," Miss Earle smiled at her. "I can see you running the fifteen hundred metres, and winning gold like Sebastian Coe. Wouldn't that be amazing?"

"I could join you at the Olympics," Jayne added. "I could be part of the equestrian team."

"Just like Princess Anne," Maxine pointed out, and turned back to stare out of the window.

Thirty years later, Maxine offered to be the liaison with Miss Earle, whilst Trudy volunteered to coordinate the publicity with Clover Bay Primary School. It was the simplest of tasks, as she relayed her demands to Jason to pass onto the lady in the school office who dealt with their media affairs.

The date was set for 26th June, which was the last Sunday in the month, just as the quiz final had been in 1981. The date was exciting to Trudy and Leon for more than the reunion and the photograph. They discovered that the latest instalment in JJ Broome's Zygon series was to go on sale at midnight on the Saturday, and the author was going to be doing a book signing in Waterstones to coincide with the launch. The pair pledged to go together.

As the moment hurtled towards them, Leon volunteered to research hotels for them to stay in the night before, but Fiona stepped in to say that she could organise a free apartment so that they could all reside together more socially. Foxhams had an apartment rental section, so her daughter Fortuna would be able to pull some strings. On reflection, Fiona realised that Ted had connections at some of the most exclusive hotels in London, and securing a discount at the Ritz or the Savoy just meant a word in the right person's ear, but it would be nicer for them to all be living together for 24 hours.

"So, that's the apartment block up there on the right," Fortuna told her mother as they strode over Vauxhall Bridge and swung right onto Riverside Walk. She pointed a manicured nail at the tall glassy tower that dominated the south bank of the Thames.

"The location's good," confirmed Fiona, spotting an assortment of casual bars and restaurants within striking distance.

"Just wait until you see the views," Fortuna added, indicating that Fiona should follow her into the serviced entrance, where she waved at the uniformed man behind his desk in the corner. "There's a pool and gym at your disposal," she continued, "and the concierge desk is staffed 24 hours a day should anybody need anything." She paused to call the lift.

Fiona regarded her fondly. "You have the Foxham knack for selling the benefits of a property," she observed.

Fortuna pulled a face to indicate that she didn't agree. "This place sells itself. And besides, it's a freebie, so I don't need to do a hard sell on it. If you don't like it, then tough. You can find your own solution." She laughed, but Fiona knew that Fortuna was desperate to have her mother's approval.

As the lift rose to the 30th floor, Fiona was reminded of the time she came to view flats with Alex. It would have been late in 1990, she calculated, twenty-one years ago, when she was just nineteen years old. It was her first proper job after college, and she couldn't believe her luck at having been successful in the job interview. There must have been other candidates who were better qualified, or with more experience, but there was something about Fiona that Alex had taken to. He joked later that he offered her the job because of her "nice rack". It probably was the truth, knowing Alex. He was barely a year or two older than her, but had been handed the responsibility of managing the Chelsea branch of Foxham's from his dad, who was busy building the estate agent empire across West London. The interview had been with just Alex, and she was attracted to his confidence, his easy manner and honesty.

"The pay is a bit crap," he had admitted within five minutes of starting the interview. "There are great opportunities to move up in the business, though."

Thankfully she picked up the tasks that were assigned to her with ease. The filing was straightforward, she had a good manner with the customers coming to buy or sell their properties, and she quickly got the hang of the Lotus 123 spreadsheet software.

"If you're not busy, you can come out and take a look at some new properties with me," Alex offered on her fifth day. "It will help you to get an appreciation of what the agents do on a day-to-day basis."

Fiona looked up from her data entry task. He looked suave in his long woollen coat and shades, waggling his car keys at her.

"Yeah, I can spare a couple of hours," Fiona agreed, thinking how refreshing it would be to escape the confines of the office, "if Alice is happy to answer the phone".

Alice agreed, and Fiona grabbed her coat, which looked shabby and aged next to the designer gear that Alex wore.

They drove east in Alex's bright yellow Mazda MX5, following the river towards the Docklands, an area under significant development. Alex gave a running commentary about the areas they were driving through, illustrated with tales of misdemeanours from his youth. Occasionally he punctuated a sentence by calling another driver a knobhead, or tooting his horn impatiently.

He parked up at Anchorage Point, on the bank of the Thames.

"Nearly all the flats have sold," he explained, leading the way towards the entrance, "but there are just a few remaining and the sales staff have moved on, so the developer wants us to flog them". He ran his eyes up the outside of the building and swept them over the river vista. "Shouldn't be too difficult. These are in a prime spot."

Fiona trotted behind him as he strode into the building's communal entrance and called the lift.

"So, what sort of price do these go for?" Fiona asked. The lift travelled up to the fourth floor where the top floor apartments could be found.

"The developer wants sixty grand, but we probably need to convince him to drop that down to fifty." Fiona whistled in awe of anyone that could pay out that sort of money for a two-bedroomed flat.

"These do have the premium river views, but the market's not that buoyant at the moment," Alex explained. He dug the key from his coat pocket and swung the front door open to reveal a space flooded with sunlight streaming in from the windows across the lounge. The smell of paint and new carpet lingered in the warm space. Even unfurnished, it felt welcoming and Fiona allowed herself to wonder if she would ever be successful enough to live somewhere like this.

She glided through the space and was drawn to the window, where a side door led out to a small balcony overlooking the grey waters of the Thames.

"What sort of people can afford these?" she asked. Alex was busy scribbling notes on an A4 sheet.

"Bankers mainly," he explained. "Usually a second home. They'll stay here in the week while they make their millions at Canary Wharf, then head back to the country at weekends. Some will be snapped up by companies who will rent them out. You just never know, but they should be easy to sell. Just look at that!" He joined her at the door and opened it so that they could go out and admire the view from the balcony. It was surprisingly quiet for London.

"So, how have you enjoyed your first week?" Alex asked as they leaned over the balcony side-by-side.

"I'm enjoying it," Fiona replied truthfully. "It's interesting, and everyone's very nice at the office."

"Good. I hope we've made you feel welcome. I'm pleased with your work." He smiled at her and to her surprise, he slipped his left hand onto the back of her thigh. "I like that you wear short skirts to the office."

Fiona was flummoxed and said nothing. He was attractive, yes, but also her boss. A little whisper in her head reminded her that he was abusing his position. She pushed the thought aside as his hand rose higher between her legs. There was no reason why she couldn't enjoy his attention.

From that day, things escalated and Alex started taking Fiona out to view properties more often, and within a week they were having sex in his car on country lanes, or in the kitchenette in the office in the early evenings when everyone else had gone home.

"Maybe we could go for dinner one evening?" Fiona asked, as she rearranged her skirt after a quickie in the bathroom of a townhouse in Chelsea.

A cloud fell over Alex's face momentarily, before he shook his head. "Let's just keep this casual, shall we? I'm not really looking for a girlfriend or anything."

"Yeah, absolutely, that's cool," Fiona replied, trying to keep the disappointment from her voice. The exhilaration of their secret affair was fading fast and it was starting to feel like he was taking advantage of her more and more. But she couldn't lose the first proper job she'd ever secured.

"Mum?" Fortuna's voice jolted Fiona out of her reverie. "Is this going to be OK for you and your friends? Just look at the view!"

What a difference twenty years made, Fiona mused. Apartments on the river nowadays cost several million pounds and came with floor-to-ceiling windows, communal cinema rooms and health spas.

"Yes, darling," she confirmed, imagining her long-lost friends cooing over the space. "This is just perfect."

17

Nina, Jayne's sister, had a boyfriend. Jayne told this to the gang as they shivered in the queue waiting to bat in the game of rounders. Only Maxine didn't care that her skinny bare legs had turned salmon with the cold, as the icy wind cut across the school playing field. She was used to running cross-country in the wintry weather now, so the prospect of Miss Earle dragging the class out onto the grass in February didn't faze her. For Trudy, Leon, Fiona and Jayne, the hour's PE lesson was torture. They jumped up and down on the spot to try and get warm.

"I haven't met him," Jayne continued. "Nina takes him up to her room and they talk in there."

"Do you think they do it?" Fiona asked. She had heard Daryll talk to his mates about "doing it" with a girl, and she wasn't quite sure what "it" entailed, but she knew it was something naughty that adults didn't make public.

"He's nineteen," Jayne replied, as though that answered the question. "Mum thinks he's too old for her, and she should be concentrating on her O-levels this year, but Dad says she's mature enough to make her own decisions."

Trudy stepped forward to bat. She missed the first time, and then made a pathetic hit on the second attempt. She dithered before making the run to first base, but was too late. The opposing team quickly tossed the ball to the fielder, who stabbed the pole on first base and she was out.

"Bad luck," Jayne called to her.

"What does 'mature' mean?" asked Leon. He still had Jayne's story in his possession at home and was determined to improve his lexicon so that he could be as proficient in writing as Jayne was. He sucked up every new word with the same enthusiasm that he collected stamps.

"Erm, kind of grown up," Jayne explained, stepping forward to take her turn at batting. Tennis lessons had been thrust on the Gray sisters since they were seven, so Jayne was confident swinging her bat and sending the ball soaring out into the barren area, devoid of fielders. She scampered around the four bases to the cheers of her classmates, getting her third full house of the match.

"I don't think the age difference matters," Maxine chipped in, when Jayne had returned to the back of the batting queue. "Prince Charles is much older than Lady Diana! Everybody seems to think it's wonderful that they're getting married, because they're so in love. It's like a fairy tale!" The nation had been captivated by the announcement of the engagement a few days beforehand, and the Clover Bay pupils looked forward to the extravaganza of the wedding in the summer.

"He's taking her out for a meal on Valentine's Day," Jayne continued on the theme of the big romance between Nina and her new beau. "They're going to the new Indian restaurant on Main Street for a curry."

"Yuk," Maxine responded. "Curry looks like sick."

"It's actually very tasty," Jayne argued. "My dad makes a lovely madras. He travelled around India when he was younger so knows how to make an authentic curry."

"What does 'authentic' mean?" Leon enquired. Jayne rolled her eyes. His constant questioning had not gone unnoticed and it was getting tiring.

"It means it's like the real thing," she replied, before swiftly adding that it was her birthday in a few weeks and she was going to have a party. She was the first of the gang to turn eleven, and her party would inevitably set the standard of birthday parties for the rest of them.

Through the pony club, Mrs Gray had managed to borrow a couple of well-behaved ponies for the weekend, so the party guests were able to have sedate rides around the paddock. Nina begrudgingly helped out, leading the ponies around the edges of the field whilst nervous ten-year-olds clung onto the ponies' manes.

Fiona was ecstatic, getting her first taste of life in the saddle. She begged Nina to be allowed to trot, but the elder sister was reluctant to take the responsibility for any broken bones on her watch.

"She's going to have to get off in a minute," Jayne observed, as Fiona requested one more circuit of the paddock. "Nina's going off on a hot date."

The arrival of the boyfriend in his swanky red sports car had not gone unnoticed and even Mr Gray emerged from the house to take a closer look. Nina thrust the pony's lead rein at Jayne and dashed to welcome her sweetheart, leaving Fiona sat on top the horse wondering whether that meant another circuit of the paddock or not.

"Oh my, is that a Lamborghini?" Mr Gray asked, as the tall, tanned man rose from the driver's seat. He lifted the shades from his eyes and peered round at the crowd of children hovering near the gate to the paddock.

"Daddy, this is Mike," Nina said by way of introduction and the two men shook hands.

"Absolutely, it's a Jalpa," Mike replied proudly. "I picked it up on

Tuesday."

"Well, make sure you drive safely when my little girl is on board," Mr Gray instructed. Nina squirmed and danced around to the passenger side to slip in.

"Wow, what a motor!" Leon sighed as the car growled its way out of the drive and onto the lane. "Mike must be very rich."

"Right kids, who'd like some sandwiches and cake?" Mr Gray asked. There was a mountain of food laid out on the dining table, from mini sausages on cocktail sticks, tiny pork pies, cheese and pineapple cubes, to cupcakes, jellies and the promised sandwiches. Fiona realised that she was ravenous enough to abandon the saddle and fill her paper plate as much as she dared. The children sat around the food, chattering merrily and watching Jayne as she opened the gifts that people had bought. Felt tip pens, a joke book, a new pencil case, a cassette of the Bay City Rollers. As the presents piled up, Fiona felt conflicted. She'd love to get all those items for herself, but that would mean having to have a party, and there's no way she'd fit many friends into her tiny lounge, let alone have her mum agree to feeding them.

"So, does she keep a diary?" Trudy asked Jayne, her voice lowered to stop Mr and Mrs Gray from overhearing the conversation. They were back on the subject of Nina and Mike, and what secrets they could discover.

Jayne's eyes widened with anticipation. "Yes, it's a blue journal. She keeps it in her bedside drawer."

"Well, let's go and get it while she's out," Trudy insisted. "We can take it down to the den and have a read and see what they get up to."

"But we're not allowed in Nina's room," Jayne pointed out, horrified.

"So, we send someone to go and get it. Someone like Maxine," Trudy conspired. "If she gets caught, she can just say she got lost on the way to the bathroom. It's the sort of dumb thing Maxine would do."

"What's that?" Maxine's ears pricked up at the sound of her name.

Trudy outlined the plan, and Maxine put her ham sandwich down in protest. "Why me? That's not fair."

"OK, we'll let fate decide," Jayne compromised. The others watched as she left the table and opened up the box of Junior Monopoly that her aunt had gifted to her, and took out the dice. "We'll all throw the dice once. Lowest number has to go and get the diary. I'll start." Primly, Jayne rolled the dice onto the tablecloth, and peered round the plate of jam tarts to see how they had landed. "Three and six is nine. You go, Maxine."

Maxine rolled two fives, and with relief realised that she had the highest roll so far and wouldn't be required to trespass into Nina's bedroom.

"Leon." Jayne hurriedly whispered the rules of the exercise and the dice were handed over. Nervously he shook them over the table and groaned as he spotted a one and a three. "Four!" Jayne announced with glee.

"Come on then. My turn," Fiona conceded. She nonchalantly threw two threes and shrugged. She was up to a spot of thieving if necessary.

That left Trudy to roll, and she could barely bring herself to let go of the dice. She cursed herself for the silly suggestion. Now she may have to pay the price.

"Two and a three," shrieked Jayne as the dice clattered to a stop against the trifle dish. "That's five, so Leon is the loser."

Leon blushed as all the girls turned to regard him. "I don't want to," he muttered.

"Oh, go on," Trudy urged, "It'll take you five seconds. Rush in the room, grab the diary, stuff it under your shirt and meet us down in the den."

"You kids having fun?" Mrs Gray interrupted proceedings. She stood above them, slotted spoon in one hand and a cache of clean dishes in the other. "Who wants trifle?"

"We're a bit full, Mum," Jayne replied casually. "Can we have some later? I was going to show the girls something down in the den."

"And I need to pop to the loo," Leon replied, steeling himself for the task.

"Oh, OK, you just holler when you're ready for some. There's even a splash of sherry in there," she added with a cheeky wink.

Without bothering to reply, the girls rose from the table and scampered off towards the stairs to the basement, whilst Leon slipped away to head upstairs to the bedrooms.

"I bet you'll have some," Mrs Gray addressed her husband, who emerged from the ground floor office where he had been wrapping the pass-the-parcel.

"You bet I will!" Mr Gray loved trifle.

"Oh, and you're back already!" Mrs Gray exclaimed as Nina and Mike came in from the hallway, and eyed the leftovers on the table.

"Yeah," Nina replied peevishly. "Mike got the time of the film wrong, so we'll have to go back in an hour."

"Never mind. Come and have some sandwiches."

"It's OK. We'll get a hot dog at the cinema. We're just going to go to my room and play some music for a bit."

Mr and Mrs Gray exchanged glances, but let them go. With a sigh, Mrs Gray attacked the trifle.

On the floor below, ten minutes passed before the girls got worried. They threw theories around between them about where Leon could have got to. Maybe he needed the toilet after all, maybe he couldn't locate the diary and was having a more thorough look around, maybe Mrs Gray had persuaded him to stay and eat more on his way back through the dining area.

"I'll go and see what's happened," announced Trudy, feeling a pang of guilt that this was all her idea. She trotted up to the ground floor where she observed Mr and Mrs Gray tucking into the leftovers at the table. Without being seen, she continued on up to the first floor, where she paused and took stock. Nina's door was first on the corridor, and it was shut, it's hostile "KEEP OUT" sign on display. There was the muffled beat of music seeping out from the bedroom, and for a moment Trudy entertained the thought of Leon playing Nina's records. As she tip-toed closer to the door she heard the laughter of an adult man rumbling from the room. Goodness, she realised in panic, Mike and Nina are in there. She glanced down the corridor to the bathroom, where the door was wide open and daylight flooded the space. No chance of Leon being there, then. She poked her head around Jayne's bedroom door in case Leon had chosen to seek shelter there. It was still and empty.

At a loss, Trudy retraced her steps back down two levels and reported her findings to the gang.

"He must be hiding - trapped somewhere - in Nina's room," Jayne calculated with a mix of awe and amusement.

Leon had indeed made a dive that would make a goalie proud at the sound of Nina and Mike's approaching footsteps on the stairs. He'd wriggled further under the bed amongst an array of long-lost socks, t-shirts, scraps of paper and dust, and lay as motionless and silent as he could. He was afraid that the sound of his thumping heart would give him away, and tried to steady his breathing.

Once they put music on, Leon allowed himself to relax a little. Mike had bought Nina an album by The Vapors, and the pair both sang along to a track about turning Japanese before collapsing into giggles on the bed. The mattress springs sagged to within an inch of Leon's nose and once again, he held his breath, praying the dusty atmosphere wouldn't make him sneeze.

He was so relieved to hear Nina suggest they make a move once side A had finished, and scampered out from under the bed as soon as the coast was clear. Diary forgotten, he went to the loo to wash some of the carpet grime from his hands, and then descended to the ground floor.

Pass-the-parcel was underway around the large dining table, and he slipped in the gap between Max and Jayne, seemingly unnoticed.

The parcel was down to its skinny last layer, and Mrs Gray let the music play until the parcel approached Fiona's hands, when she pressed pause. She was standing with her back to the table, but had been watching proceedings in the mirror, so enabled the music to pause at strategic points to give every child a chance to remove a layer and do a forfeit.

Fiona shrieked with joy as the music stopped with her holding the parcel. She ripped off the colourful paper and gasped as she realised that this was the last layer, and she would keep the treasure inside. A brand-new pack of thirty felt tip pens, arranged in a rainbow. She'd never owned new felt tip pens before, and hugged them to her chest, remembering to thank Mr and Mrs Gray graciously.

"Leon, you haven't got a drink," Mrs Gray observed. "Can I get you something?"

Leon blushed, not only because Mrs Gray's eyes were on him, but because of the weight of expectation from the gang who were desperate to hear what had occurred in the quest for the diary.

"May I have some Coke please?"

"Oh, we don't have any Coke in the house, I'm afraid, but we do have orange juice and apple juice?"

Leon frowned in confusion. He'd clearly just heard Nina and Mike discussing the amount of Coke that was being stored in the tack room. There was loads of it apparently, so why couldn't Mrs Gray just go and get some from there? He was powerless to challenge, though, as he shouldn't have been hiding under the bed and eavesdropping in the first place.

"Oh. I'll just have some orange juice please," he replied politely.

18

Fiona was dreading Alice leaving for the evening as that meant it would be just her and Alex left alone in the estate agency. He'd probably want a quickie in his office, and this behaviour was frustrating her. She really needed this job. She loved it, and she was desperate for the money, so was reluctant to say no to having sex with her boss. She hated herself for her weakness, but felt she had no choice.

She had only been working at Foxhams for a month, and could imagine her mum's wrath if she went home to say she'd lost the job. The cost of renting property in London was too steep for Fiona to contemplate moving out, but she was proud to be able to pay a contribution for her bed and board.

Alice slammed the desk drawer shut, shaking Fiona from her reverie.

"Right, that's me done," she announced. "I'm off." Fiona watched as Alice tugged on her jacket and bid her farewell.

Silence fell and Fiona wondered how long it would be before Alex emerged from his office at the end of the showroom and ask if she wanted to pop in for a minute. And it would only take a minute, she thought savagely.

She sat glumly at her desk, staring at the traffic crawl along Sloane Avenue. It was getting dusky, the end of what had been a promising spring day. She approached the door to turn the sign around to display that they were now closed, and watched as a burgundy Jaguar pulled up outside, putting on his hazard lights as though that made his illegal parking OK.

"Knob," she muttered under her breath, but curiosity made her stand and observe the culprit. The driver emerged from the car. He was in his forties, but already his mop of thick hair had turned silver. Under his tweed jacket she spied a cravat spilling out from his shirt, which made him look like a bigger knob in Fiona's estimation. Her heart sank as he strode purposefully towards the door, his face full of thunder.

She took a few steps back to the safety of her desk.

"I'm afraid we've just closed," she said brightly as he burst through the door. She wished Alex would give her the keys so that she could lock the door properly at six o'clock, but as the last one to leave, Alex preferred to secure the premises himself.

"Well, you'll just have to stay open for a few more minutes to sort out my problem then, won't you?" the man barked at her. There was a northern hint to his accent, but she could tell he was a posh twat. Someone who was used to always getting his way.

"Certainly, Sir," she agreed, hating that the customer was always right. Supposedly. "How can I help?"

"It's my gaff," he replied, as though she should know exactly which one of the hundreds of properties was his gaff. "You guys have had it on the market for four weeks now and it's not sold, and you've hardly had any viewings, and I want to know what you're gonna do about it?"

"Well, Mr...," she paused, waiting for him to fill the gap, but nothing came. "Let me look up the records and see what we can do about it. Your name was?"

"You've had four bloody weeks to do something about it, and it's not good enough. I want to see the manager. Now!"

His voice was bouncing off the walls to the extent that Fiona knew Alex would be out to see what the commotion was about.

"Certainly," she repeated with a calm smile. "I'll go and fetch Mr Foxham. Who shall I say is..."

The door to Alex's office opened and he emerged. To Fiona's confusion, his face broke into a grin.

"Leave the poor girl alone, Dad."

Fiona looked back to the customer, whose features had been fully transformed as he smiled generously back at Alex. His eyes now twinkled behind the thick frames of his glasses, and his posture relaxed.

"How long have you been hiding this one?" he asked Alex, jerking a thumb towards Fiona.

"Dad, this is Fiona. She's been with us for the past month. Fiona, this is my dad, Mr Foxham. Senior," he added needlessly.

"Edward," he corrected, his hand shooting out to shake Fiona's. "But you can call me Ted."

Fiona shook his hand politely and looked between Alex and Ted with momentary confusion. "So, do you have a property for sale with us?"

Ted threw his head back and gave a hearty laugh. "No, sorry about that. I was just messing with you. I like to drop by and see what new staff are like with customers under pressure."

"Oh," Fiona blushed. It seemed both father and son liked to take advantage of her good nature.

"You passed the test," he added gently, and touched her reassuringly on her shoulder. "I just dropped in to go over some business with Alex," he explained. "But if you're still here when I'm done, I don't suppose you fancy heading off for a bite to eat? I like to get to know the staff better."

Fiona hesitated. This family were very forward.

"If you've got other plans, it's not a problem."

"No, I'm free. That would be nice," she heard herself saying. It would be better than having to endure having sex with his son.

Half an hour later, Ted held open the passenger door for Fiona to clamber in. Miraculously the car hadn't been punished with a parking ticket in the time it took Ted Foxham to do his business with Alex. Ted chattered about the perils of driving around West London as he eased into the traffic and Fiona was relieved at how easy it was to be in his company.

She hated to admit to herself how wrongly she had judged him on first impression. He wasn't a knob after all, just very sure of himself. From the old-fashioned clothing to the way he greeted the staff at the Savoy like old friends, he was comfortable in his world. Fiona was concerned that she was under-dressed for the hotel, and fiddled nervously with the hem of her short skirt as she sat on the velvet banquette seats in the bar. The waiter swooped in and handed them a menu the size of a phone directory, which Ted put to one side. He wasn't to be rushed into ordering. He asked for a cosmopolitan, and Fiona panicked. Aside from a payday alcopop, or a sneaky cider with Darryl, she'd barely dabbled with alcohol, and had no idea what drink would be appropriate to order in this situation.

She glanced around at the other customers and ordered a white wine to copy the lady to her left.

The waiter opened the leather-bound menu to reveal a lengthy list under the heading 'Wines by the glass'. A jumble of French words swam in front of Fiona's eyes so she glanced over to the corresponding price. Bloody hell, even the cheapest was a couple of hours of her salary. She pointed to one, not daring to pronounce it, and prayed that Ted was picking up the bill.

"Good choice, Madam," the waiter praised, and Fiona held back a smirk. Nobody had ever called her madam before, except her mother when she was cross with her as a child.

Over drinks, Ted told her about his upbringing in Yorkshire where his dad ran an estate agency in a small market town. It was successful and, when he retired, he offered the business to Ted. Out of duty, Ted ran it for a few years but his father soon passed away, and Ted no longer felt a duty to stay in Yorkshire. He saw the potential of replicating his dad's success in London. He figured that he could focus in on the high-end market, where this would net the biggest gains. London was transforming, with property prices soaring through the 1980s, and an estate agency that took a slice of the sale price was riding high.

In return, Fiona told him her shorter life story about growing up in Clover Bay, moving to London with her mum who had struck up a relationship with a new man, and starting work at Foxhams.

"I trust Alex is treating you well," Ted stated with a warm smile. Fiona nodded politely. "He's a good boy," he continued fondly. "He works very hard and I'm lucky that I can trust him to look after the branch while I expand the business."

The waiter interrupted their conversation to escort them to their table in the dining room. A pianist tinkled the ivories in the corner of the restaurant, and the noise of the bar faded away, leaving civilised quiet and the occasional chink of cutlery.

Fiona ordered soup and steak, the two items on the menu that she was confident she would like, and Ted asked the waiter to recommend a bottle of wine to complement the steak.

"I hope you're not planning to drive after all this alcohol," Fiona commented once the waiter had retreated. One of Darryl's friends had wrapped his car around a lamp post in Clover Bay after drinking five pints and attempting to drive home. The police said he was lucky to escape with just a broken leg and concussion.

Ted shook his head. "I'll get a room and stay here tonight," he confirmed. "I keep an overnight bag in my boot just in case. Besides, I have to go and see some associates in the city tomorrow so it makes sense to stay in town."

Fiona marvelled at the grandeur of the hotel and wondered what the rooms were like. "Do you have a suite like Richard Gere had in 'Pretty Woman'?" She asked. She was captivated by the movie and had seen it twice at the cinema last summer.

"If I do, will you be my Vivian?" he joked, placing his warm hand over hers. Instinctively she pulled her hand away, and regarded him with distaste. What was wrong with these Foxham men, thinking they could just treat her like an object? Like father, like son, it seemed.

"I'm sorry," he gushed hastily. "I was just trying to make a joke."

Fiona regarded him warily. "What would Mrs Foxham think about all this as she sits back at home?" she challenged him peevishly.

Ted appeared to sag. It was the first time she had seen him look vaguely defeated, but she refused to feel sorry for him.

There was an awkward silence momentarily before Ted sighed.

"You're right. Mrs Foxham is at home. She's buried under the cherry blossom tree in the garden."

Fiona fell silent as the waiter chose the inappropriate moment to come and pour the wine. He methodically displayed the bottle to Ted, removed the cork and poured a tiny amount for Ted to try. He sipped at the wine and nodded for the waiter to fill up their glasses. It had given Fiona time to process his words.

"She died?" she asked once the waiter padded away from the table again.

"In 1980," Ted confirmed. "She contracted pneumonia at Christmas and there were complications. She passed away quite quickly."

Fiona mumbled that she was sorry. She cursed herself for judging him so quickly.

"It left me to bring up the kids on my own," Ted continued. "Poor Alex and his sister were still in school, so it was hard on them to lose their mother so young."

"Well, you've done a good job of it," Fiona praised. "My mum had to bring up me and my brother on her own." She sensed that Alex and his sister weren't brought up in a council house with a rusty freezer dumped amongst the dandelions on the front lawn. There was probably childcare of some sort bought in rather than leaving the kids to put frozen pizza in the oven and get high on cheap fizzy drinks.

Ted raised his glass to her, a smile breaking through the momentary shadow on his face. "To you, Fiona. Welcome to the Foxham family."

Fiona chinked her glass against his and smiled back.

19

The day of the quiz final in London fell on Fiona's 11th birthday, which meant she was relieved of the expectation to have a party. This would be the best outcome, Fiona figured, as everyone would still make a fuss of her on her special day but she wouldn't have to beg her mum to put on a party, feed a herd of hungry youngsters nor be embarrassed that her party wasn't a patch on those held by her friends.

Since Jayne's birthday party in March, the other members of the quiz team had turned eleven. The twins were able to make use of the skittle alley in the back of the pub to hold their party, and their parents had pulled in a range of favours to get a mobile disco running and a buffet to feed the 5,000. Leon elected to have a picnic on the farm for his birthday, and the classmates sprawled on blankets amongst the daisies in the meadow, before learning how to milk a cow, playing hide and seek in the cavernous barns, and racing up the mountains of stacked straw bales to see who could reach the top the quickest. Maxine outran them every time.

There was one obstacle to overcome to ensure Fiona could avoid holding a party, and that was winning the semi-finals of the quiz championships. To be held in Exeter, there were six teams competing to win the opportunity to represent the south west region in the London finals. A six-to-one chance meant that Miss Earle wasn't confident of it going in their favour.

The Clover Bay Echo sent a giddy junior reporter over to the school the day before to interview the quiz team and Miss Earle. She asked predictable questions about whether the team were nervous, and how were they revising, whilst Miss Earle confirmed how proud she was of them to get this far. Miss Earle had no expectations about the Clover Bay team getting through to the final stage. The competition was stiff, with a team from a prestigious boarding school from Devon, as well as representation from a private school with a formidable reputation for excellence from Dorset.

In addition to the four members of the quiz team, the minibus had space for Mr Gray, who was keen to take in some of Exeter's architecture, and Mr Riley, the PE teacher. Maxine, clutching Hector the lucky mascot, wasn't to be left behind, of course. The adults took the front seats whilst the pupils sat thigh to thigh on the benches in the back.

As they travelled along the M5, Mr Gray created quiz questions using place names on signage and passing vehicles as inspiration.

"Dad, we're going to be all quizzed out by the time we reach Exeter," Jayne complained after yet another question. This time the question concerned the link between a red car travelling in the inside lane and Texas.

"Come on, this one's easy!" Mr Gray protested.

"It's an Austin Metro," Jayne relented.

"And…?"

"And Austin is the state capital of Texas."

"Excellent, and can you name three other cities in Texas?"

"Maybe we should let the kids rest," Mr Riley interjected, throwing a sympathetic smile towards the gang huddled on the hard bench seats that ran along the sides of the minibus.

"Ah, you're not tired, are you, kids?" Mr Gray asked, not expecting nor waiting for an answer. "We could do some math questions. Such as…," he paused to ponder briefly. "It's the thirteenth of the month today, and somebody's birthday is on the thirty-first. How many days is it until their birthday?"

"Whose birthday is it?" Maxine asked eagerly. She liked it when somebody had a birthday.

"It's Jason Easton's birthday on the thirty-first," Trudy piped up.

"Who?" Mr Gray asked, irritated that his line of questioning was being derailed so quickly.

"Jason Easton," Jayne replied. "He's in our class." She managed to keep her response casual, despite her heart thumping in her chest. Jason was the best-looking boy in class and Jayne was determined to make him fall in love with her. She watched him bring her words to life in the school Nativity just a few short months ago, and hoped that he noticed her as she excelled in the role of narrator, looking professional and studious, and never once messing up a line. She'd been conscientious about praising Jason every time he did a good job, and in the euphoric surge of completing a word-perfect dress rehearsal, she had spontaneously flung her arms around him and bear hugged him for as long as she could before he pulled away.

"Yay!" Trudy had joined in, grabbing Jayne for a hug, then turning to Jason and embracing him, jokingly referring to him as "her husband". His face lit up and he giggled. Jayne turned away, annoyed at the jealousy she felt as she witnessed their interaction.

The trouble was, Jason seemed to be more interested in Trudy, and this infuriated Jayne. In Jayne's eyes, Trudy wasn't anything special and she struggled to understand what Jason saw in her. She was plain and uninspiring.

The Gray children were used to getting what they wanted. Look at Nina, and how she had secured her rich, attractive boyfriend. Even her father approved of Mike, the glamorous boyfriend with the flashy sports car. Her dad would definitely approve of Jason, with his steady approach to life, his easy-going manner and generous smile. She adored his smile.

Now that she had discovered his birthday was in a few weeks - well, eighteen days to be precise, as she finally reported back to her father to satisfy his need for a quiz answer - she could buy him a birthday gift and card. He hadn't acknowledged the valentine card that she sent him, but comforted herself with the knowledge that the card had been anonymous. It was a fantastic specimen that she'd made herself out of red card, flower petals from the rose bush in the garden, and tissue paper. She'd spent a whole Saturday creating a rose on the front and composing a rhyme for the inside. Surely, he would have guessed it was from her; nobody else could write powerful prose as she could. It read: "Roses and red, Violets are blue, Joseph was a saviour and you could be too."

She'd placed a massive question mark beneath her rhyme and embellished with a few love hearts in shades of pink and red around the border of the card.

It only struck her after all that effort that she wasn't sure how to get it to him. She didn't know where he lived, nor how to find out. She could try to slip it into his bag in the classroom but the potential for being caught in the act was too risky.

In the end she confessed her predicament to Trudy as they sat in the corner space of the classroom working on a list of points to debate around "If you could wish for anything, what would it be?".

Trudy had started to list out reasons for ending gun ownership. The shooting of John Lennon in December had really upset her mum, and there was a lady in the pub that started crying when the news went around. Trudy couldn't think of any reason why guns shouldn't be banned.

"So, what are you going to wish for?" she asked Jayne, noticing that her classmate was staring into space, her paper blank before her.

Jayne leant forward conspiratorially. "I'd wish to go on a date with Jason Easton," Jayne whispered to Trudy, "but I guess I can't make that my actual thing to debate".

"You like Jason?" Trudy whispered back to clarify. She had no idea, and knew it was a doomed infatuation. Jason cruelly referred to her as "the brat" during the rehearsals for the Nativity. Never to her face, of course, and now in light of this confession, Trudy felt a little sorry for Jayne.

"He is sweet," Trudy concurred.

Jayne nodded. "I've made him a valentine card, but I don't know how to get it to him." She glanced around and checked Miss Earle wasn't looking their way before reaching into her bag and sliding the fat, pink envelope onto the table.

Trudy admired the silky paper whilst giving it some thought. "Well, his dad drinks in my parents' pub every Saturday after the darts match. I can ask my dad to give it to his dad if you like. You know, he can just say it's from someone at school."

Jayne's eyes lit up, excited that there was a solution. "You'd do that for me?"

"Of course," Trudy replied. She hadn't expected Jayne to acquiesce so easily. For someone so bright, Trudy doubted that Jayne had fully thought through the potential consequences of this plan.

Thirty years and three children later, it would seem Trudy's suspicions were right.

20

As June drew closer, Fiona raised the question about whether partners or other family members should attend the reunion weekend. Whilst Ted was no longer around, she was keen to show off Fortuna to her former classmates. She had no qualms about sharing a double bed with her daughter, and knew that Fortuna, with her confidence, beauty and intelligent input, was not what the Clover Bay contingent would expect of her. She was also curious to meet any woman that Leon had managed to secure, and take a look at Grant, who had been described in one of Trudy's emails as "good-looking, but with a swagger that borders on arrogance".

"I spend all week in the smoke. Why would I want to spend a weekend there as well?" Grant protested when Maxine broached the invitation.

"It's only one weekend," Maxine responded, hurt that he would rather rattle around the cottage on his own than spend precious time with her. "I thought you might want to meet my school friends."

Grant peered over the top of his magazine. From the image of the glassy office block on the cover she could tell it was one of his property development magazines.

"You'll have more fun without me," he concluded. "Besides, I need to tackle the garden."

Maxine couldn't argue with that. Their regular gardener had gone into hospital for a knee replacement operation and the warm days and frequent downpours meant the garden was quickly resembling a jungle.

Leon didn't even bother to consult Sasha. There was the problem of her greyhound; he knew it would be an issue to find someone to look after Droopy, and selfishly he needed her to be in command of the business for the weekend. It was hard enough for him to leave, but both of them? Impossible.

"Well, I can't go," Jason pointed out, when Trudy remarked that Maxine was asking Grant to come to London. "Somebody needs to stay at home to look after the human dustbin." He nodded towards Robbie, who was raiding the hall cupboard in search of a packet of crisps.

"Why can't we all go?" Robbie suggested, his ears pricking up as he realised what they were discussing. "I've never been to London."

"There won't be room for all of us, love," Trudy replied gently.

"Fiona's kindly organised the accommodation and there's only one bedroom each."

"But JJ Broome is signing the new book that weekend. I don't need a bedroom. I could sleep on the sofa. Please!" He rarely begged for anything, but Trudy knew it wasn't fair to burden her adult friends with an eleven-year-old. She promised Robbie that she would queue at midnight and get him a signed copy of the book, and that once he'd broken up for the summer holidays, perhaps they could all have a weekend in London as a family and see the sights.

As for Miss Earle, she lived in London so had no need to stay in the apartment, and arranged to have drinks and a meal with them on the Saturday night, before reconvening on Westminster Bridge for the photo on Sunday morning.

Everything was set, and Fiona found herself excited as she woke on that Saturday morning. Fortuna was meeting her at the apartment block with the keys at two o'clock, so she had all morning to wait. She'd already picked out what to wear, having tried on every outfit in her wardrobe earlier in the week, and been to Waitrose to buy a range of fizz and nibbles.

Leon planned to drive from Clover Bay to London and agreed to give Trudy a lift. It sounded like a straightforward arrangement, but Saturday mornings were a blur of chaos in the Easton family, and took military timing to ensure Robbie was dropped off at football practice, before Jason delivered Trudy up to Leon's farm and returned to pick up Robbie and run some chores for work.

Leon was nowhere to be seen when Trudy arrived, so she stood self-consciously near the till in the shop whilst an employee went off to hunt him down.

"Sorry," he called to her across the shop a few minutes later. He was still adorning his butcher's apron, with blood smears visible across the navy and white stripes. "Just got a couple of issues to contend with. Won't be a tick."

Trudy waited patiently, shifting her weight from one leg to another, consulting her watch as the minutes ticked by. Finally, he emerged again, shedding his apron. "Sorry about that. One of the toilets wouldn't flush, and then we've got reports of a bee's nest in the tree in the car park. We'd better get out of here before the next disaster strikes."

"You don't want to change?" Trudy asked, looking him up and down. His faded t-shirt had splashes of goodness knows what speckled across it, and his blue jeans were so old and worn that the colour had faded to a shade of lavender.

"I'll change when we get there," he promised, raising his holdall to indicate that he at least had a change of clothes. "Let's get on the road."

It felt strange at first sharing a lift with Leon, who was all but a stranger to Trudy. Thirty years had changed them both as adults and they made small talk, struggling to find a topic where there was common ground. Neither had travelled much, Trudy didn't follow football, Leon didn't have kids, and the only mutual friends they shared were the ones they were about to spend the weekend with. Trudy hoped conversation would be easier when there were more of them.

Maxine had been organised. She looked back on the photo from 1981 and suggested to everyone to wear a navy outfit as similar to that day as they could find. She wasn't in the photograph, but on closer inspection, she saw that Hector was. Trudy held the lucky mascot in her right hand, his little felt dog face turned to the camera. Maxine knew that she would never have got rid of Hector, so he must be in one of the boxes in her loft. When her parents sold up and relocated to a retirement property in Spain, Maxine had the task of clearing all her childhood junk from the pub. For several years the boxes sat as spare room junk, but had recently been relocated onto the newly acquired boarded floor of the loft. Cross-legged, Maxine began to work her way through each box, distracting herself with memories along the way. In a box of books, she discovered the 1981 Jackie annual, and a smile crossed her face and she flicked through the pages and remembered discussing the articles with Trudy. They learnt to tell if a boy loved them by his facial expression, what their choice of favourite pet revealed about them, and an A-Z of making the most of yourself. The astrology section advised readers what colour they should wear according to their star sign in order to make them most attractive to boys.

Maxine didn't need the book to tell her not to wear red, which clashed against her vibrant hair colour. She could just about get away with wearing shades of orange but had to match against her foxy hair with care. For this evening she had chosen a black silk Japanese dress that accentuated her curves and made her feel powerful. It had splashes of colour across it, which could be used to match her accessories.

Putting the annual back in the pile, she unearthed more photo albums. There were grainy images of toothy seven-year-olds taken at summer camp, and several family snaps of Christmas dinners in years gone by. Each picture evoked a smell or memory of Maxine's happy childhood. She reluctantly stowed the albums back in the pile and reached for the smaller box behind it. Emblazoned with the "Smith's salt and shake" logo on the outer, it was a relic from the pub, and even that brought back the recollection of her parent's storage shed in the corner of the pub garden. It was where they stashed the surplus stock, and stupidly didn't have a lock on the door. Trudy and Maxine frequently raided the crisps, stuffing packets up their jumpers and then running the gauntlet to get back to their bedroom unseen. Their parents must have known that they were the thieves, although they accused customers, and even foxes, of breaking into the store.

This box contained an array of ornaments and nick-nacks that Maxine would never display as an adult but was too sentimental to discard. There was a small white china horse that Fiona had given her for her birthday, with an apology that she'd had to nick it off the market. Somewhere along the way its front leg had shattered, so it no longer stood up. Maxine wasn't sure why she'd kept hold of the Mickey Mouse keyring that her Aunty Margaret had brought her back from Disneyland. She'd been extremely jealous of her aunt for having the opportunity to go there, and pissed off with her parents for saying they couldn't afford the time nor money to take Trudy and Maxine.

Then her heart leaped. Beneath the failed pottery attempt, the slightly balding teddy bear of her infancy, and the broken Bros alarm clock, she glimpsed the grubby grey body of Hector the beanie dog. He'd lost his glassy right eye at some point in time, but there he was. The lucky mascot. She hugged him to her chest with a satisfied sigh, then put him to one side to take to London.

A flash of green caught her attention at the bottom of the box and, moving aside the naked Sindy doll, she pulled out her childhood jewellery box. The delicate pattern on the lid had faded from the years that the box had endured hours of sunlight as it adorned her chest of drawers. She lifted the clasp and opened the lid, but the ballerina inside no longer fired up to twirl to a tune. Maxine remembered that there used to be a key in the back of the box that she would wind up to make her spin, but the key was lost long ago. She could still remember the way the tinny tune of Lara's Theme made her sway. How did it go, she mused? "Somewhere my love, la la la la la la," she sang to herself as she picked through the dated pieces of costume jewellery that had been consigned to history.

She pulled open the narrow drawer at the base of the box, and drew out something wrapped in tissue paper. As she peeled back the delicate layers, she suddenly remembered what lay beneath. It was Jayne's glass necklace that she'd accidentally put in her pocket all those years ago. She blushed with shame, but couldn't help admiring its beauty as she freed it from the wrapping, and held it up to the dusty light. The block of aquamarine glass was encased into a silver setting, and it was mesmerising.

It would look fantastic with the black silk dress that she was wearing Saturday night. She placed the necklace next to Hector ready to give these pieces of history their moments of glory once again.

21

Fiona stared at the stack of boxes on the shelf in Boots, her heart thumping. Partly it was through embarrassment of having to take the packet up to the till. She was sure the shop assistant would silently smirk to herself that this customer had potentially got herself up the duff. Mainly the nerves were for the result. A baby. At her age. If she were ten years older, it would be perfectly natural to be seeing whether she was expecting a baby. A wanted baby with her loving husband. The school prophecy of being the most likely to have a bun in the oven before marriage seemed to be coming true. OK, she was twenty and not sixteen, but still only casually shagging her boss who seemed to have no intention of making their relationship anything more concrete. The frustrating thing was that she thought she'd been careful. Alex too; he was always insistent on using condoms, and would be horrified to discover her news. He had foil packets stashed in jacket pockets and his desk drawer the way other people always had chewing gum to hand. Fiona knew that nothing was ever one hundred percent effective, and if anyone was going to catch that narrow chance of misfortune, it would be her.

Then there was Ted, of course. Following their first encounter at the Savoy a month ago, Ted continued to sniff around like a dog on heat. Fiona was unable to stop herself being drawn to him. He was a true gentleman. He was rich, confident, paid her compliments and despite herself, she was falling for him. She liked him enough to allow him to take her to dinner again, and this time agreed to go and see his swanky penthouse suite at the hotel. It was like the scenes in Pretty Woman, she decided, with views out over the rooftops of central London, and a bathroom that sparkled clean. They'd continued to drink champagne in the suite and, when Ted moved in to kiss Fiona, she melted into him, feeling safe and wanted. Unlike the hurried sex of his son, Ted never assumed anything, and it was Fiona who took the initiative, seductively peeling off the layers of his clothing and leading him to the bed with its crisp, clean sheets with their floral fragrance and velvety texture. Ted repeatedly checked she was OK, and Fiona reassured him that she wanted this. She wanted him. She wanted the experience and maturity of this man who was twenty years her senior. Age meant nothing. This felt right.

A week later, the glamour of the penthouse behind her, she grabbed the cheapest box and shuffled to the till, keeping her head down as she paid. It was her lunch break so she'd have to hurry back, not that Alex was in today, but Alice was holding the fort while she was out. She scuttled back to Foxhams and thanked Alice, who promptly put on her jacket and vanished for her own break.

Fiona sat at the desk, staring out at the street where happy workers and tourists passed. Everyone seemed to be chatting and carefree. Every now and then she would glance down at the paper bag protruding from the jaws of her handbag. She should probably get it out of the way and do the pregnancy test now. It'll be fine, she told herself. She'd used protection with Alex, and it was too soon after Ted for that to be a worry. She was just late, that's all.

But she wasn't late, and to her horror the blue line appeared on the stick and mocked her.

"Fuck," she swore as she stared at the evidence, praying that somehow that line would fade away again. Tears welled up and spilled down her cheeks as a waterfall of jumbled thoughts rushed into her brain. What now? Why her? Shit, shit, shit.

She threw the stick into the bin and stared at the reflection in the mirror. What a mess. Her face was now puffy and her tears had ruined her eye makeup. She tried to pull herself together, knowing that she was supposed to be holding the fort whilst Alice was out, but every time she thought she could hold it together, another sob would escape her throat and fresh tears leaked down her cheeks.

Finally, she forced herself to think other thoughts and returned to the office. There was a mountain of paperwork to be sorted and filed. She could distract herself with that and pretend the last thirty minutes hadn't happened.

When Alice returned, Fiona ducked her head lower behind her computer monitor and pretended to be reading some printouts.

"Watch out," Alice warned. "Boss is coming."

Fiona glanced up, expecting to see Alex approaching the door, but her heart sank as Ted's burgundy Jaguar sat on the double yellow lines outside with the hazard lights on. Whilst an unexpected visit from Ted would be nice under normal circumstances, today was not a good day for him to see her.

"Good morning, ladies," his Yorkshire tones broke the silence of the office. "How are we on this beautifully sunny day?"

"Very good, Sir," Alice confirmed. Fiona found it strange to hear her lover being called Sir.

"I've just popped in to grab some papers that Alex has left out for me." Fiona kept her head down as Ted approached, but she sensed him pause as he reached her desk.

"How are you, Fiona?" he enquired.

She glanced up and registered his jolt of surprise as he witnessed her messy face. She tried to give a smile, but feared it was wonky.

"I'm OK," she managed to reply, but the concern etched on his face only made her feel on the brink of more tears. She willed him to just nod and carry on through to Alex's office. Most men would. Instead, he crouched to her level and lowered his voice so that Alice wouldn't hear.

"You don't look OK to me. You seem a little bit peaky. Are you sick?"

"No, no...I..," she desperately wanted to tell him to go away and leave her alone, but this was her boss. She couldn't lose this job on top of everything else.

"Let me take you home," he interrupted. "I insist. Come on." He rose back to full height and held out his hand to her. Fiona glanced at Alice, who was unsuccessfully pretending not to watch the proceedings.

"Alice, I'm taking Fiona home. She's not well," he explained. "I trust you'll be OK holding the fort?"

Fiona couldn't tell whether Alice was annoyed or bemused as Ted led Fiona out of the office and held the passenger door open for her to climb into the leather seat. She hoped she could repay the favour to Alice one day.

"So," Ted said as he nosed the car into the stream of traffic. "Where shall we go?"

Fiona thought of the down-at-heel streets of Newham where she shared a cramped terraced house with her mum and her beau, Reg. She suspected that the shoe repair shop and the loan and thrift society building on the Barking Road were a far cry from Ted's world. He shouldn't be expected to drive his swanky car around those parts.

"I live in East London, so just drop me at the tube station. It'll save you going out of your way when you're busy."

Ted glanced over at her. He had a conspiratorial look on his face.

"I bet you don't want to go home, do you?"

That was true. Despite the sunshine, the house would be cold, and she'd only mope around within its woodchipped walls feeling miserable.

"We can go anywhere," he continued. "Let's play hooky. I am the boss after all!" He grinned at her, and was pleased to see that she was smiling back at him. "What about the seaside? We could head for Brighton and walk along the seafront. Ooh, what about having some fish and chips and scoff them out of the paper? Loads of salt and vinegar."

"I grew up by the seaside," she replied. "It doesn't hold much appeal to me."

"Well in that case, have you ever been to Kent?"

"I haven't really been anywhere," she confessed.

"In that case, I know where we'll go."

Fiona let herself be driven through the core of London and recognised that they were heading south. She began to relax in his company and the chat flowed easily. He hadn't asked any more questions around how she was feeling, and she was grateful for that. For now, she could just pretend that this morning hadn't happened.

The landscape outside turned leafier as Ted drove through the green suburbs of south west London, before finally joining the M25 motorway. All three lanes were busy, and Fiona wondered how people endured this slow snaking journey every day.

"Are you taking me to Gatwick?" she asked, seeing signs to the airport.

"Not today," he laughed, "but maybe we could have a romantic weekend in Paris sometime?"

Fiona's heart leapt. This showed he was anticipating a long-term future with her. Paris would be amazing! She'd have to get a passport first, but then there was a whole world that they could discover together. She'd never been abroad. Any holiday, let alone a foreign holiday, had been out of reach for her mum.

She was starting to wonder how much longer she'd have to endure the endless tarmac, when Ted flicked the indicator and pulled off the motorway.

"Seriously, where are you taking me?" she persisted.

"This, Fiona, is Sevenoaks," he announced proudly. Looking out of the window, she saw the outskirts of a respectable town. The houses dotted along the suburban road were detached and set back from the carriageway by neat driveways, before breaking to reveal bowls clubs, recreation grounds, or just patches of trees. This was a far cry from Newham.

"What's so special about Sevenoaks?" she asked, although the evidence was right outside her window.

"Me!" he replied with a chuckle. "It's where I live. The garden of England. Look, that's a wonderful nature reserve," he pointed to an expanse of grass to the left with a rippling lake bordered by a crowd of trees.

"It looks lovely," Fiona swooned.

"I moved here mainly for the golf course, which is just down the road from me. One of Kent's finest. We celebrated its centenary last year. Ooh, I love my golf," he added needlessly. Fiona could see how animated he had become.

"I guess you remember it opening then?"

"You cheeky madam," he scolded, giving her a playful thump. He turned down a country lane, where the spaces between the driveways became further apart, indicating much larger plots for the homes that resided out of sight. "I have some very wealthy neighbours," he explained, waving his hand vaguely towards hostile looking gates. "There are a few swimming pools and tennis courts on this road, so I hope your expectations haven't risen too high. I'm a Yorkshireman. I don't waste money on extravagance."

He slowed and turned into a gravel drive, and Fiona got her first glimpse of Rose Cottage. It wasn't vast, but the red brick facade looked proud and well kept, with bulging hanging baskets adorning the porch.

"Welcome to Rose Cottage," Ted announced, unclipping his seatbelt and glancing at Fiona's reaction. "It was already called Rose Cottage when we moved in. I wanted to call it "Teed Off Cottage" - you know, because of the golf - but Diana wouldn't let me."

Two minutes over the threshold and the dead wife gets a mention, thought Fiona with a tinge of bitterness. She clambered out of the car and followed Ted on the gravelled path that wrapped around to the back of the house. The rear garden was stunning. She ran her eyes over the manicured lawn that covered the size of two tennis courts, bordered by tall, mature, bushy fir trees that screened the garden from neighbouring properties and swayed drunkenly in the breeze. In the centre of the lawn was the cherry blossom tree that Diana's ashes were buried under. It was in peak bloom, giving the garden a pink focal point.

A wide terrace traversed the back of the house, complete with barbeque, a smart wooden table for entertaining and a retractable umbrella, folded up and redundant this time of year.

"You've got Knole Park over there," Ted pointed beyond the hedge, "Sevenoaks Common just down the road and we're less than half a mile from the High Street".

"Once an estate agent, always an estate agent, eh?" joked Fiona. He didn't need to sell this place to her.

"Anyway, it's a bit parky out here. Let's get inside and have a brew."

She checked her watch as they went from the terrace through the door to the kitchen, and wondered what plans Ted had for the rest of the afternoon. The kitchen had the neat, orderly air that suggested Ted didn't use it much. She couldn't imagine him cooking up meals for one, and presumed he had a cleaner that would drop in periodically to ensure the residence continued to look cared for. There was even a vase of fresh daffodils on the farmhouse table in the centre of the kitchen.

"Go on through to the lounge and make yourself comfortable," Ted instructed as he busied himself with the kettle.

She made her way into the hallway, pausing briefly to take in the surroundings. An aged grandfather clock stood to attention in the corner, its pendulum swaying steadily in contrast to the frenetic sound of Ted whistling in the kitchen.

Seeing spotless cream carpet beyond the boundary of the lounge, Fiona kicked her shoes off, and entered. Like the kitchen, it looked untouched, and somehow staged. A couple of burgundy three-seater sofas were angled around the fireplace with a bare, polished wooden coffee table in the centre. The aroma of furniture polish hung in the air. There were a range of ornaments on the mantelpiece, and Fiona began to wonder whether Ted had brought her to one of his portfolio homes that was on the market rather than his own house. It was the sort of joke she could imagine him playing on her.

With relief, she spotted some family photos on the occasional table in the corner. On closer inspection, one showed a studio portrait of the family of four: Ted, Diana, Alex and what must be Ted's daughter, assembled carefully in front of the photographer's lens. Alex looked about twelve in the image, with his sister a couple of years younger. Fiona scrutinised the image of Diana to see what legacy she had to live up to. Diana looked warm and carefree. She smiled as though Ted had just said something cheeky to her. He probably had. Although the photo must have been taken at least a decade ago, Ted didn't look any different. His gentlemanly outfit was timeless, and his hair was already grey back then.

"Here we go," Ted brought the mugs of tea into the lounge and placed them on the coffee table. "The family gallery," he needlessly explained, joining Fiona to peruse the pictures. "That was 1980," he confirmed, "and is probably the last photo of Diana. God, you just never know what's around the corner, do you?"

"You must miss her." Fiona knew her words were inadequate but had no idea what else to say.

"Of course. She was my first love, and I never thought I'd want to date again. I couldn't even contemplate the idea. And I didn't for a long time, and by the time I felt I was ready, everyone my age was either taken, or on their second time around with complicated baggage. That's the hard thing about being widowed in your thirties."

"At least you have golf," Fiona pointed out after a respectful pause.

Ted smiled appreciatively at her and nodded slowly. "Yep, at least I have golf. And someone to play truant at work with. Are you hungry?" His attention was suddenly diverted, and Fiona realised that she hadn't had lunch, and was indeed hungry. "We'll have our tea then walk down to the town. I know a lovely little bistro."

"Ah, you have some vinyl!" It was Fiona's turn to change the subject as she spied a record player on the stand near the doorway. "Can I?" she asked, flicking through the block of LPs waiting in their purpose-made wooden box next to it. Madness, Vienna, Shirley Bassey, Showaddywaddy,

Gary Numan. Fiona was pleased to see that their musical tastes aligned. This was the soundtrack to her childhood.

"Pop something on," Ted invited.

It didn't take long for Fiona to choose. The black and white cover of The Specials album took her straight back to the 80s, to the cassettes that Daryll nicked from Woolworths. Somehow, she didn't envisage Ted or Diana running out of the shop with this stuffed up their jumper.

"Oh, cracking choice!" Ted praised, looking up from where he had sat on the sofa to sip his tea.

"I can't not dance to this," Fiona confessed, feeling the beats of "Message to you Rudy" run through her veins. Without embarrassment, she bopped around in the corner of the lounge, her eyes closed, with the vague recollection of doing this with Jayne when she came to sleep over that time. There was no soft carpet under her feet back then. Ted watched her, enthralled.

"Come on, join me," she urged as the second track came on. "Do the dog," she sang tunelessly whilst bouncing from foot to foot.

"Not the donkey!" Ted sang back, suddenly remembering the track. What the hell. He rose to his feet and began to bounce alongside her, the incredulity of ricocheting around the lounge like children at three o'clock on a Monday afternoon making him giggle.

He grabbed her hands and pulled her into him, hugging her tight so that they jigged as one unit.

"Oh God, Fiona," he breathed, nuzzling her neck. "I love spending time with you. You make me feel young again."

Fiona loosened her grip on him and leaned back to look him in the eye.

"You're only as young as the woman you feel." It was corny, but summed up the situation as Ted's right hand found its way up inside her blouse.

"Exactly," he whispered.

The bistro was forgotten and the tea went cold.

22

"I think if you turn left down this next street, you can get to the underground car park that way." Trudy was feeling under pressure as she attempted to interpret the sat nav, read Fiona's instructions and navigate for Leon, who was getting uncharacteristically stressed. The wide London roads with cars, scooters and bicycles on all sides were a far cry from driving around the country lanes of Clover Bay.

"I can't. It's one way. Look, "no entry" signs," he snapped.

"Well, can you take the next left and see if you can loop back around?"

Leon's eyes darted from his mirrors and over his shoulder, trying to manoeuvre into the left lane to make the turn. He managed it just in time, receiving an angry blast of a horn from a bus coming up on the inside. He was glad they were nearly there. Thankfully, they'd landed on some common ground on the three-hour journey when Trudy started talking about books. Leon described his love of science fiction and, once they remembered their shared passion for the Zygon series, they were able to dissect the nuances of the five instalments so far and speculate about what was going to happen in the concluding sixth novel when it was launched later that day.

"I'm just as excited to be meeting JJ Broome," Leon admitted. "He's such a recluse apparently and very few people know what he looks like."

"I wonder who's already arrived," Trudy mused as she relaxed, knowing that the chaotic streets were behind them, and they only now had to potter around the quieter side streets to get to the building.

Fiona had already arrived. She had told everyone else that the check-in time was three o'clock so that she could arrive an hour earlier, assign herself the best bedroom, stock the fridge and finalise her appearance. She had only just managed to get the last bottle of prosecco into the fridge when there was a knock on the door. Fiona checked her watch and felt a wave of annoyance that it was only half past two. Why couldn't her friends follow instructions?

"Maxine!" she exclaimed. Her brain processed the same glossy red hair, the slim build and the classy clothing before the friends gave each other a tentative hug. "You haven't changed a bit."

"Nor you," Maxine replied, although she noted the ageing on Fiona's face. More striking was how she'd managed to move on from her council estate roots in the cut of her clothes, the way she held herself and the waft of her expensive perfume, which Maxine detected in seconds.

"This place is amazing," Maxine gushed, taking in the London skyline momentarily as Fiona waved her through to the living space. "Imagine living here. I don't think I'd ever tire of that view."

She'd barely had time to offload her own stack of wine onto the kitchen island and place her suitcase in the twin bedroom when there was another knock at the door.

Leon and Trudy entered the apartment looking weary from their drive but elated to be reunited with the gang again.

Fiona fussed around them, directing them around the property. By the time they had circled back into the living space, Maxine had already opened and poured the first bottle of fizz into flutes and emptied a packet of cheese straws into a container that she found in a cupboard. Hosting was one of Maxine's fortes.

"Well, cheers!" she toasted, as they hovered around the kitchen island, grasping their flutes. They chinked each other's glass and took a gulp, all desperately hoping that they would find their natural rhythm as adults as they did thirty years ago.

"Here's to…"

Maxine paused. She wasn't sure what the ultimate objective of the get-together was. Yes, they would go and take a photo on Westminster Bridge tomorrow, and hopefully have a pleasant evening later, but why had she really done this? She'd got so swept away with the idea of a reunion that she had lost sight of what, if anything, she hoped to achieve from it.

"To a successful twenty four hours?" Trudy filled in for her.

"And to us," Leon added.

"To us," they all chorused. It seemed a good enough toast.

"What a shame Jayne's missing, though," Fiona lamented. "I couldn't think of any other way of searching for her."

Everyone nodded in agreement.

"What do you remember most about her?" Trudy asked the group.

"God, Trudy," Maxine retorted. "We're not at a wake, trying to make polite conversation about the deceased."

"Well, it's the one thing we all have in common," Trudy replied, stung. She got annoyed at Maxine when she went into group social mode, swishing around like the queen bee.

"I think it's a good question," Leon piped up, perching his buttocks on a bar stool. "I remember what a great writer she was, for her age. I was so jealous because she knew all these big words and could combine them into colourful sentences. Here I am at forty one and I still don't have the vocabulary she had at ten." He glugged back the last of his drink and could feel it warming his belly. He hardly drank at home and, combined with the release from the drive into central London, he was starting to feel giddy.

"Do you remember that writers' circle she set up?" Leon continued. "It was after we wrote the Nativity, we all got together at hers and had to write a story. I think we only ever met once under that guise because none of you lot would take it seriously."

"I only ever remember us meeting at her place, though," Maxine said, moving to the fridge to fetch a top-up for Leon's glass. "Considering we lived at a big pub, I don't recall you lot coming round to ours except for our birthday party."

Fiona thought about the time she led Jayne to the twins' pub garden to raid crisps and fizzy pop from the garden store in the early hours but decided to keep quiet. Stealing from your friends wasn't the sort of thing to blurt out after so long apart.

"I remember her pony," she offered. "And her sister's boyfriend with the sports car."

"Oh yes, her sister, Nina!" Leon exclaimed, a sudden recollection flooding back to him. "I remember being trapped under her bed. What had I been doing? You lot sent me upstairs to hunt for something in her room and they came back, so I dived under her bed and prayed I wasn't going to sneeze."

He paused to acknowledge Maxine as she refilled his glass, and took a hearty swig of replenished bubbles. "This is going down really well," he enthused.

"It's proper champagne," Maxine explained. "None of this prosecco muck. Grant always insists on champagne when we entertain."

"Nice if you can afford it," grumbled Trudy, who had tucked a bottle of prosecco in the fridge.

"Well, I'm just more used to beer," Leon admitted. "I've never been a big drinker."

They all sipped at their flutes and glanced around at each other, all still amazed that they were together again.

"Do you think we were good friends to Jayne?" Fiona said suddenly. "I don't know about you, but looking back it feels like we were all take, take, take from her. I feel a bit bad that we might have abused her kindness. And her parents' generosity."

Maxine's hand slipped up to grasp the glass necklace around her neck, and realised Fiona may have a point. Trudy glanced at the wallpaper on her smartphone. It was a picture of Jason smiling down the lens from his seat at a wooden table in a pub garden. It was summer and he was relaxed and happy.

Leon blushed.

"I have a confession," he stated. The three girls all looked at him expectantly. He wriggled uncomfortably on the stool, wondering whether he should admit this.

"Oh yes?" Maxine urged him to elaborate.

"If it wasn't for Jayne, I would never have had the money to build the farm shop." There. He had said it out loud for the first time. The girls all regarded him blankly. It was clear they needed him to elaborate. "Oh God, where do I start?" Leon stifled a giggle, thinking back to the dirty deed. "You remember the first and only writers' circle evening? Jayne had written a fantastic short story about a guy at a book club that turned out to be an alien." The expression on everyone's face suggested that Leon was the only one to remember the occasion over thirty years ago. He continued. "Well, I took the story home with me. I just wanted to study the vocabulary she'd used and the way she put sentences and dialogue together. It wasn't really stealing, well not in my head it wasn't, and I was going to give it back to her." He paused to finish off the champagne in his hand. "I kept it, and a year or two later, I submitted it to a junior writers' competition in my science fiction magazine. In my name," he added for clarification. His cheeks flushed the colour of a strawberry. He still felt uneasiness about the fraud, and never ruled out the possibility of being found out. "The story won first prize, of course. It was a brilliant story for an eleven-year-old to write. And I won a hundred pounds. That was quite a lot of money back in the eighties."

"Not enough to fund a farm shop, though," Trudy pointed out, remembering how the confession started.

"No," Leon continued. "I was in a predicament as the prize money was paid by cheque made out to my dad, Mr J Batty. As a junior entrant, I'd had to forge my dad's authorisation on the entry form, so then I couldn't tell him I'd won because he'd probably have made me send the prize money back to the magazine or something."

"Why did you forge his permission in the first place?" asked Fiona. "Couldn't you have just told him you were entering?"

"I wanted to keep it under the radar, I guess," he replied. "I knew I was entering a story that wasn't mine so didn't want anybody in the family to know. I went to the building society where my parents had set up a savings account for me, and told the cashier that they had made a mistake on the cheque and put a J instead of an L, and they believed me and paid it in, and allowed me to take the £100 in cash. I remember having the bunch of bank notes on me as I went home. It was like being in possession of a stash of crack cocaine. I was paranoid the police were going to tap me on the shoulder and ask where I'd got the cash. So, I put it in a box at the back of my chest of drawers and didn't touch it for years. In the back of my mind, there were a thousand scenarios, like I thought the Gray family may return to Clover Bay, or Jayne may read the winning story in the magazine and recognise it as hers."

Leon paused. He felt as though he was talking far too much and wanted to hear about Fiona's life over the past couple of decades.

"Well, finally after at least ten years, I realised that nothing was going to unravel and it was probably safe to spend the money, but there was nothing I particularly wanted to buy. The National Lottery had just started, so for a laugh, I bought a hundred lucky dip tickets. It was a bit of an experiment, you know, wondering whether I would break even." He laughed at the memory. "Well, yes. I not only broke even but I managed to bloody match five numbers and the bonus ball!"

"Wow!" Trudy's eyes widened in amazement. She'd religiously played the lottery once a week and only had the odd ten pounds winnings here and there. "How much did you win?"

"Fifty thousand and ninety pounds. That was a lot of money in the nineties."

"It's a lot of money now!" Trudy swooned.

"So that windfall funded the conversion of a couple of our disused barns into the deli and farm shop, and the rest is history. I just told my dad I'd bought a single lucky dip ticket, and got lucky. The thing is, I would never have bought a lottery ticket if it wasn't for the money I'd got from Jayne's story, so effectively my whole livelihood is all thanks to her."

The gang regarded Leon in awe. He blushed and shifted awkwardly in his seat. "Anyway, enough about me. I'm dying to hear what Fiona's been up to in the last twenty years."

23

Fiona and Ted had become inseparable, with many mid-week overnight dinners. Overnight stays at swanky West End hotels were a regular occurrence. In the Foxhams office, Alex sensed something was up. Fiona avoided situations to be alone with him and, as Fiona's belly started to swell, she knew she was going to have to make some decisions.

Her mum swayed between devastation, anger and love as Fiona confided in her first.

"I just didn't want you to turn out like me," she groaned as they sat together at the shabby garden table. It was a metal bistro set that had been left by the previous tenants when they moved into the property, and Fiona noted how rusty and dirty it was. Everything in their tiny back garden was in stark contrast to Ted's place and galvanised Fiona's ambitions for the future. She'd given her mum an edited version of events, neglecting to mention her liaisons with Alex, and instead focussing on the fairy tale romance with Ted.

"I prayed you wouldn't be as stupid as me, lumbered with a baby at such a young age, unmarried and without a proper career," her mum continued, lighting up her second cigarette in fifteen minutes.

"At least I know who the father is," Fiona retorted cruelly. It was also a lie, but Fiona had decided to create her own truth.

"Yes, your boss! Bloody hell, Fiona."

They sat in silence as sirens wailed in the distance. Fiona doubted you'd hear a siren from Ted's garden.

"You definitely want to keep it? It's not too far down the road if you wanted to get rid."

"Yes, I'm keeping it," Fiona snapped bluntly. That was not up for discussion. "Ted's a good man. He'll look after me."

Her mum looked doubtful. She'd had her share of bad experiences with unreliable men, and wished her daughter would approach with more caution. Dating someone her age would be a start.

"Well, you'd better tell him then, hadn't you?" She stubbed her cigarette out and stood up, pausing to regard her daughter. "And when can me and

Reg meet him?"

Her mum had a point, she reflected. In just six months there would be a baby, and if she and Ted were going to play happy families, their relationship needed to be out in the open sooner rather than later. Alex and his sister needed to know, and her mum and stepdad needed to be involved.

Ted was enthusiastic a few days later when Fiona suggested making their relationship official. It was a balmy July evening and he met her from work to have a walk along the Thames.

"I wasn't sure whether you were embarrassed to tell people that you were knocking about with an old codger like me," he joked.

"Of course I'm not," Fiona replied, linking her arm into his. "Age is immaterial." She wanted to tell him she loved him, but couldn't quite force the words off her tongue. "We have so much fun," she said instead.

"If Alex and Angela are free on Saturday night I can invite them over to mine for a dinner party?" Ted suggested. Fiona decided to tell him about the pregnancy after dinner, once he'd had plenty of wine and some scotch, just in case he wasn't as delighted by the news as she hoped.

To Fiona's surprise, Ted was a talented chef and had planned a three-course meal cooked from scratch. He picked her up and drove her back to Sevenoaks, parking on the high street to pick up provisions from the butcher, greengrocer, florist and wine merchant. Everyone serving in the local shops treated him like a long-lost friend, asking after him and his children, noting how nice it was to see him.

Back in the kitchen, Ted spread the provisions out over the counter tops.

"I haven't told Alex you're here, or what this is about," he explained as he pulled an apron over his shirt. His summer wardrobe was as smart as his winter attire, swapping tweed jackets for Italian linen, and leaving off the cravats in favour of bright spotty handkerchiefs in the breast pocket. He regarded Fiona through his thick rimmed glasses.

"I'm looking forward to meeting Angela," Fiona replied. In reality, she was apprehensive about meeting his daughter who was more or less the same age as her. How would she react to the news that her dad's new girlfriend, the one who would stand to inherit everything ahead of her and Alex if they were to get married, was just in her twenties too? Never mind the news about them being an item, Angela and Alex would also have to stomach the news very soon that their dad was having another baby. That would make her baby a brother or sister to Alex and Angela, Fiona calculated with a lurch of nausea.

For a fleeting moment, Fiona considered an abortion to be the most logical step, but she galvanised herself and offered to help.

They made a good team, with Fiona taking instruction from Ted. She decanted the wine, arranged an array of flowers into their vases and spread them around the reception rooms, chopped vegetables and laid the table.

"Ah, there's five of us," Ted pointed out spotting the four placemats on the table. "Plus, a spot for Barney."

"Barney?"

Ted looked at Fiona as though she was daft. "Alex and Katrina's son," he prompted.

Katrina? Fiona's mind whirled. Alex had a family??

"Alex has never mentioned his home life," she explained. "The office chat is strictly professional." A wave of outrage welled up inside her. The little shit. "He has a wife?"

"Yeah, he's been married to Katrina for four years now," Ted said, smiling proudly. "She's a lovely girl, very sweet. And little Barney came along eighteen months ago. He's into everything, you know, the age where he's toddling and you have to watch him like a hawk."

That makes him the nephew to my unborn child, calculated Fiona, feeling sick again. This was blowing her mind. She gripped the back of the wooden farmhouse chair and took a deep breath.

"I think I'll go and get ready," Fiona said, desperate to be alone to process this news. "They'll be here soon."

She scampered up the stairs and into Ted's bedroom. She'd learnt not to think of it as Ted and Diana's bedroom now, and Ted had respectfully removed photographs of Diana from the bedside now that Fiona was sharing the bed regularly. She didn't yet feel like it was her bedroom, although she had been given a drawer that she stowed underwear and toiletries in. She stood at the window and gazed out over the lawn. She was dreading the dinner party even more now, having to face Alex with his "sweet" wife who was completely unaware of the blatant way Alex had taken advantage of her. At least that was in the past now, and it gave her the upper hand.

Pulling herself together she made an extra effort with her hair and make-up, chose a short dress that exposed a decent amount of cleavage, and steeled herself as she heard the crunch of car tyres on the gravel below.

From the top of the stairs, she heard the commotion of families coming together. The chatter, the laughter, the joy as Ted scooped up his grandson and twirled him in the air as he squealed in delight. It was a sound Fiona had never had in her childhood and she craved it now.

She descended the stairs slowly and hovered in the kitchen doorway like a shy virgin.

Alex sensed her presence and turned to face her, his eyebrows shooting up in surprise. "You're the last person I expected to see in my dad's kitchen."

"Fiona's been helping me out today," Ted explained, handing the restless toddler back to the sweet looking girl.

"Dad," Alex scolded. "It's a Saturday and this is way beyond Fiona's job description." He introduced Fiona to Katrina without any embarrassment. Fiona shouldn't have been surprised.

Angela arrived shortly after by pushbike, a step-through frame with wicker basket on the front. She was surprisingly un-Foxham, wearing student-style dungarees with paint stains streaked across the thigh. It transpired that she had graduated from art college and was now living in locally in a shared flat, earning money by being a barista and selling artwork from a community gallery in Brighton.

Ted introduced Fiona as "his friend" to which Alex added that she worked in the Chelsea branch. Fiona wondered at what point the grand reveal about her being Ted's girlfriend would happen. It certainly wasn't going to come with the whirlwind of excited chatter as they poured drinks, exchanged the latest news, and had an aperitif sitting in the wilting sunlight in the garden.

Fiona managed to avoid the alcohol without drawing attention to it. She poured herself soda water and passed it off and a gin and tonic, then as the wine started to flow with the food, she poured some fizzy apple drink and claimed it was a white wine spritzer.

The main course came and went and, just as Fiona sensed an appropriate pause for Ted to reveal his news, Barney started to get tetchy and was put to bed in a cot in the spare room. The moment seemed to have passed, and Ted brought out dessert and then coffee.

"So," Ted said finally as the coffee cups were drained and a bottle of scotch appeared on the table. He reached out and put a warm hand over Fiona's. "Fiona's not just here to help out. She and I have been seeing a lot of each other lately. Romantically," he added for clarity. Fiona stole a glance at Alex and Angela who were both wearing stony poker faces. "I guess you could say she's my girlfriend. We're dating."

Alex was the first to shake off his silence. "Dad, please, she's barely out of nappies."

Fiona's hackles rose. She was old enough for him to rip her knickers off in the office kitchen, though, she thought spitefully.

"She makes me feel young again," Ted replied, smiling broadly at Fiona. "She makes me laugh, and smile. Whilst no-one will ever replace your mum, I'm sure you want me to be happy."

Katrina was the only one smiling back at Ted. "I think it's lovely that you're dating," she confirmed.

Ted nodded. "Thank you, Katrina. What do you think, Angie?'

His daughter was swirling her whisky around in its glass, staring into its depths. She shrugged without looking up. "If you're happy, then that's fine. I'm not calling her mum, though."

That was the hard part of telling the kids, Ted thought, unaware of the bombshell that was coming later. Fiona was exhausted by the time she had Ted back to herself. It had taken a while to bundle Barney into the car without waking him, and wave drunken Alex and sweet Katrina off. Then a protracted argument ensued between Ted and Angela about her getting home safely. She insisted on riding her bike, whilst Ted was adamant that he should call her a taxi. She won and pedalled off down the lane as she had done a thousand times before.

"Well, that seemed to go OK," Ted observed, locking the back door behind his daughter's departure. "I'm shattered, though. Coming up the wooden hill?"

Fiona hesitated. She had to tell him, but her nerve was wavering. She could wait until the morning, but...

"Ted, I think I'm pregnant," she blurted. It was like stepping off a cliff and once the words were out of her mouth, she felt a little exhilarated and relieved.

"I beg your pardon," he replied, slumping down into the dining chair next to her. He stared at her. He had heard, but this wasn't soft, loving Ted.

"No, I don't think, I know I'm pregnant." Her heart started to thump.

"And you decided to wait until this moment to tell me."

Fiona opened her mouth to reply but had no idea what to say. She closed it again and shrugged meekly. She couldn't fathom what Ted was thinking, but there had been an edge to his voice that matched the dark cloud that had come over his face.

"What do you want from me?" he asked. "Money for an abortion?"

"Of course not!" she retorted, horrified that he'd think that. "I was hoping it wouldn't change anything."

"Wouldn't change anything?" Ted stood up again and started to pace around the kitchen, fists balled at his side. "We embark on this new relationship together with someone else's kid in tow?"

"Don't be silly, Ted, it's your baby."

He paused mid step and regarded her warily.

"It's your baby," she repeated, as much to convince herself as Ted.

"I very much doubt that," he countered. "I had a vasectomy in 1985. My family was done. I wanted a future with no more kids in it."

Fiona's heart lurched. She'd not anticipated any such curveballs. Her head spun and she took a deep breath.

"Nothing is a hundred percent effective." Tears started to prick at her eyes as she felt her whole rosy future slipping away thanks to her stupidity.

"No, but it's pretty much thereabouts."

"Which makes this a pretty remarkable conception, don't you think?" She was aware that her voice had started to plead, but she couldn't give up on this. "Look, I haven't slept with anyone else, Ted," she lied. "Why would I? What do you think I am, a slag?"

A sob rose to her throat as she realised that was exactly what she was.

"Oh God, Fiona, I'm sorry," Ted caved in, pulling her off the chair and into his arms. She sank into his comforting hug and let her messy tears escape into his shirt. "I don't think that at all. I'm just a bit stunned, that's all."

They stayed still in their embrace, surrounded by dirty dishes that would all have to be washed up the following morning.

"I suppose we'd better think about making you Mrs Foxham," Ted murmured in her ear. "We can't have you having a child out of wedlock."

It wasn't the romantic proposal that Fiona had dreamt about as a little girl, but it was the best she could expect after the way she had acted.

24

It was nearly time to meet Miss Earle. She had elected to choose the restaurant and nominated it based on its striking distance from the apartment. The restaurant had newly opened and was set in the former home of the Duke of Brunswick. According to Fortuna, everyone was talking about the quirky interior and the exceptional menus. She also warned that it may be pricey and everyone would need to look smart.

The expense worried Trudy, who had a finite limit of cash in her purse. Maxine was grateful for the opportunity to be glamorous and admired her reflection in the long mirror in the bedroom. The black silk Japanese dress had been the right choice. She slipped Jayne's turquoise glass pendant around her neck and was pleased with the way the light shimmered off it.

Leon wore the only smart pair of black trousers he possessed and a plain shirt. He didn't own a tie and hoped it didn't matter. His money was as good as anyone else's.

The group made their way along the riverside and followed the directions to the venue. It was a beautiful evening, with enough warmth left in the air not to need jackets. Thanks to the alcohol consumed since arriving, blood pumped through their bodies like the soundtrack to Rocky.

"There's Miss Earle," observed Maxine, spotting a slender blonde lady waiting patiently at the gate. She turned to face the gang and beamed, sunglasses hiding her eyes but every part of her posture and energy took Maxine back to 1981.

"Hi, Miss!"

"Well, look at you all," she smiled.

"You've barely changed a bit," Leon said.

"You have!" she laughed, observing the tall bulk of Blusher Batty and his bushy beard.

There was a moment of hesitation as everyone wondered whether it was appropriate to hug, or whether they should shake hands.

"Have you been waiting long?" asked Trudy, breaking the awkward pause.

"No, only a few minutes. So, let me check… We've got Leon," she pointed at Leon, who confirmed she'd got the easy one correct. "Fiona?"

She tentatively asked Fiona. Whether she was surprised to find the rough council estate girl now wearing a Boden tea dress, she didn't give a flicker away. "And the twins… Trudy."

"The less glamorous one," Trudy tried to joke, but everyone brushed her comment away.

"And Maxine. I love your dress."

"Thank you." Maxine blushed at the compliment, feeling giddy as though she were on a first date. "Do we call you Miss Earle?" she joked.

"Susie, please. I left Miss Earle back in Clover Bay a long time ago. Shall we go in?"

They followed their former teacher into the old-fashioned gloom of the restaurant, where a smart-suited host greeted them, checked their reservation and led them to their table.

"Ted would have loved this place," Fiona sighed as they settled into their places. She opened her heavy, leather-bound menu and glanced around the group. "We ate out such a lot. He loved food. Ted was my husband," she added for Susie's benefit.

Trudy had heard the story of the fairytale romance of Fiona and Ted back at the apartment and so tuned out of the conversation, reading the fancy words in front of her with a rising sense of panic, and more alarmingly, noting the prices that accompanied each dish.

"What's everyone's preference for wine?" Maxine asked, brandishing the wine list. "I usually find the best policy is to disregard the cheapest option and go for the second or third wine in the list."

"Except they aren't listed in price order," pointed out Fiona, looking over Maxine's shoulder. "They're listed by country, and then region. I prefer white, but I really don't mind what I have. Ted was the wine expert; he always chose well."

Maxine wanted to point out that Ted wasn't here. She was getting fed up of hearing about super human Ted, and was reluctant to let his ghost dominate their evening.

"I think I'll stick to tap water," Trudy stated, hoping that they weren't going to split the bill evenly at the end, making her fork out for wine she hadn't drunk. If she had one course and water, she probably had enough cash.

"I'm definitely having steak," Leon said. "Living with a vegan means I don't often get to indulge in a decent slab of cow. And I want this meal to be on me. No arguments!" he added as the girls began to make noises of protest. "You remember what I confessed at the flat? This is my atonement. Of sorts."

Everyone looked embarrassed in the British way when money is the topic for discussion. Fiona tried to protest, but Leon pointed out she'd done such a good job in sourcing the accommodation, and it was least he could do.

"So, what was the confession?" Miss Earle asked, once the waiter had returned and taken their order.

Leon blushed and waved it away. "Oh, it's a long story." One that he didn't want to repeat to his former teacher.

"Look who I found," Maxine interjected, pulling Hector from her handbag. "On the original photo, Trudy had him in her hand."

"Oh my God," Trudy gasped, reaching out across the table for the scruffy toy dog. "You kept him all these years. What was his name? Henry?"

"Hector."

"We stole him from the library if I remember correctly," Trudy added with a giggle. The wine was starting to get to her.

"You stole him," Maxine corrected. Holding court, she regaled the tale of the episode in the Clover Bay library to the best of her memory.

"I never had you down as petty thieves," laughed Miss Earle. "You were all the brainy ones, the studious ones, the brightest of the year. You wiped the Westminster School out of the water!"

"It's funny, isn't it," Maxine replied, "that I was the one who wasn't clever enough to make the quiz team, but out of all of you, I'm the only one who went to university." She swept her butter knife around the table accusingly.

"Anyone can get a third-class degree in aerobics," giggled Trudy, parroting their dad's description of Maxine's studies.

"It was three years of hard work!" Maxine protested, stung by her sister's put down in front of her peers.

"Well, if we're all making confessions, then I have something to add," Miss Earle said. The gang fell silent and all eyes were on their former teacher. "It's something I was a bit uneasy about for years afterwards, but I must admit, I feel a lot better knowing that my actions didn't impact on you as adults."

"What?" asked Maxine impatiently.

"You may remember that to get into the quiz team you had to complete a series of questions. When I came to mark them, Maxine scored the same as you, Trudy, and I think Fiona. It turned out that she was bright enough to compete."

"No way!" Trudy shot back. "Why didn't you put her in the team?"

Before Miss Earle had chance to answer, they realised that Maxine's shoulders were shaking. The sniggers that escaped her mouth became louder until she was laughing hard.

"That's so funny," she managed to splutter. "I only scored the same because I stole Trudy's answers and copied them onto my sheet!"

Trudy looked horrified momentarily, but then saw the lighter side. Miss

Earle breathed a sigh of relief.

"It was a good thing that I chose *not* to put you in the team then," she admonished with a grin. "It didn't stop you from achieving academically, so that's good."

"I've got a degree from the university of life," added Leon. "That was a lot of toil too."

"So," Fiona spoke up. "If Leon stole Jayne's story and Trudy stole Hector, what did you steal as a ten-year-old, Maxine?" asked Fiona, waggling her glass of wine towards her friend. "There must have been something."

She didn't have to respond straight away as the waitress arrived with their starters, breaking the rhythm of the conversation. The wine was making Maxine bold too, but she hesitated, her hand rising to the Murano glass that adorned her neckline. Once they'd all bitten into their food and made appreciative noises, Maxine decided to confess.

She told the group of the events leading up to her shoving the necklace in her pocket, stressing that she was panicking and always intended to put it back. "But I never got the opportunity and then forgot altogether. I only unearthed it a few weeks ago when I was looking for Hector."

"I don't think I'm shocked anymore," Miss Earle responded. Maxine was relieved. It was such a long time ago. "Who else has something to confess?"

"I stole Jayne's boyfriend and ended up marrying him," offered up Trudy. "Well, to be truthful, Jayne wasn't actually going out with him, but desperately wanted to be his girlfriend. She had such a crush on him." She described how she had engineered for Jayne to entrust the valentine's card with her to pass on via Jason's dad. "Then she did the same with a birthday present for him. This time, she had signed the card, so I'm ashamed to say I destroyed the card and replaced it with my own, passing the gift off as being from me."

"That's worse than nicking her necklace," Fiona judged, but grinned at Trudy to show she wasn't truly shocked. "It all worked out too, right? Three kids, you said?"

"Three brilliant sons," Trudy confirmed.

"We really were quite cruel to Jayne, weren't we?" Fiona reminisced. "I desperately wanted her to be my best friend purely so that I could get some free rides on her pony." She paused as she finished her pate starter and pushed the bone china plate away from her. She turned sideways to Miss Earle. "Are you sure you don't know what happened to the family when they disappeared that summer? Even the ponies had vanished when we all went up to the house. I mean, surely the school would have been told?"

Miss Earle shook her head and shrugged. "It was the school holidays and Jayne was due to go to Tolchester Grammar School in September.

Once the term ended, she wasn't the school's responsibility anymore."

"So, did you get many free rides?" Leon prompted, bring the conversation back around.

Fiona smiled. She briefly recalled the wet, miserable morning at the Tolchester gymkhana where it was Mrs Gray who had behaved like the friend to her, whilst Jayne made Fiona feel as though she was just getting in the way. Dropping hints hadn't worked, and it had been impossible for Fiona to get herself invited over without the gang in tow.

Except for the night of the quiz final. She'd had her equine experience that night. She'd just had to help herself, that was all.

25

Susie Earle had allowed the children to consume too many sugary foods, but she didn't care. Technically they weren't the responsibility of the school anymore, although they were entrusted in her care for the day. The exhilaration of winning the quiz final meant that she bought them all ice creams after the photoshoot on Westminster Bridge, and allowed them to buy as many sweets in the newsagents as they liked for consumption on the train ride home.

The passengers unfortunate enough to share the same carriage had to endure the gang singing their made-up victory song as far as Southampton, followed by endless chatter.

Susie tried to shush them on numerous occasions but finally gave up, flopping back into her seat. Blocking out the chatter of the children, she stared out of the carriage window replaying the conversation with her ex in her head.

It was still light when the train pulled into Clover Bay. Trudy and Maxine's mum had left her position behind the bar to come and greet the twins, and stood outside the ticket office expectantly. It wasn't far for them to walk back to The Five Bells but it was past eight o'clock, and you couldn't be too careful these days. Jack the Ripper had been all over the news for the past few months, and made women wary about going out at night. She was joined by Mr and Mrs Gray. She recognised the pair from the school sports day she'd attended a few weeks prior. Mrs Gray was hard to miss. She was impeccably turned out and made the twin's mum feel dowdy in comparison.

"Are you here for the kids returning from London?" Mr Batty asked the group. He'd been rushing and was out of breath by the time he arrived at the platform. "I thought I might have missed them."

"You're OK," Mr Gray confirmed, checking his watch. "I think this is it coming in now."

They watched as the train crawled towards the buffers. This was the end of the line.

The train doors opened and a variety of passengers spilled onto the platform, but there was only one unmistakable group of children careering excitedly towards the exit.

"We won, we won!" shrieked Maxine as she spied her mum waiting patiently.

"You did?" Mr Gray tried to hide his disbelief and glanced at Susie Earle's face for confirmation. "Well, that's tremendous! Good job, guys!"

"We haven't got the trophy with us because they have to engrave the school's name on the metal bit," gabbled Trudy, "and then it gets sent to the school. Miss Earle says that it will go on display in the cabinet in the reception area so that everyone can see it. We got certificates and this man from the press took our photo near Big Ben and is going to make sure the Clover Bay Echo get a copy to print".

"Right, well let's get you two home," urged the twins' mum, conscious that she should be helping out behind the bar. She thanked Miss Earle, prompting Mr Batty to steer Leon away from the group and towards his badly parked Land Rover.

"Is your mum coming to get you?" Miss Earle asked Fiona, realising that all the passengers had now dissipated, leaving an empty station.

"Well, said she was," Fiona lied, "but sometimes gets called into work. I can walk home. It's OK. It's not far."

Mr and Mrs Gray exchanged glances.

"We can wait with her," Mrs Gray offered to Miss Earle, and after a round of pleasantries, the matter was settled, and Miss Earle waved goodbye. She realised as she started up her Ford Escort that that was the last she would see of the team, as they were now on their summer holidays and heading to secondary school in September. She never dreamed she'd be having a night out with them thirty years later.

"Why don't we just run Fiona home?" Jayne suggested to her parents after they'd waited five minutes. The sun had dipped behind the roof of the ticket office and her bare legs were cold.

"Yes, let's do that," Mrs Gray agreed, thinking that it would be nice to get home. "We'll keep an eye out in case your mum passes us along the way."

Fiona knew that her mum wouldn't drive past because her mum was never instructed to meet her from the station. Thinking that her daughter had been invited to spend the night at the Grays' house, she was merrily having a night with her best friend in Tolchester.

"My mum's car isn't here, which means she must be at work," Fiona observed as they pulled into her road. "But that's OK. She won't be long, I'm sure. I'll be fine on my own."

Jayne's parents exchanged uneasy glances. They felt a responsibility for her.

"Maybe your brother is in?" Jayne suggested.

"Why don't you go and see if he's in?" Mrs Gray urged. "If he's not, then we'll take you back to our place."

"I don't want to be any trouble," Fiona protested.

"You're no trouble," Mrs Gray confirmed.

Fiona nodded and hurried up the path, slipping into the hallway, where Darryl was sat on the bottom stair rolling fags in his nicotine-stained fingers.

"I thought you were staying with that posh girl tonight," he grunted without looking up.

"I am," Fiona smiled. "They just don't know it yet."

She hovered in the hallway, judging the time it would take to look as through she'd checked the house for mother or brother. When she went back to confirm that the house was empty, the Grays were adamant she should return to their home.

"Leave a note for your mum so that she knows where you are when she does return," Mr Gray instructed.

"We'll get home at some point tonight," Jayne grumbled as Fiona once again strode up her path, and entered back into the house to pretend to leave a note.

"Now what?" Darryl griped.

"I'm pretending to leave a note for Mum about where I am."

"But she already knows."

"Exactly. That's why I'm pretending."

Darryl shook his head in exasperation. "I don't get you."

A few moments later, Fiona bid her brother farewell and climbed into the back of the car. Jayne's mum went into full hostess mode, asking whether the girls were hungry, as there was a chicken casserole in the oven at home.

Fiona made the most of the food on offer, and then the girls played games in the basement den as the night grew dark.

"I can't understand how a mother can virtually abandon a child like this," Mrs Gray observed in hushed tones to her husband as they washed the dishes together. "It's nearly nine o'clock, and Fiona could be anywhere."

Mr Gray nodded in agreement. "She'll have to stay the night here, but I've got a good mind to report her mother to social services." He checked his watch, even though he was aware of the time. "She's still not called, so I guess she's not at home yet."

There was one more step in Fiona's plan before she could secure her place in the spare room bed. She needed to make a pretend phone call home, with a fake one-sided conversation to the dial tone. Mr and Mrs Gray looked on, trying to work out what kind of scenario was unfolding.

"Yes, I'll ask them but I'm sure it'll be OK," Fiona told the static down the phone line. "See you tomorrow." She replaced the trim phone receiver and turned to smile at Jayne's parents. She prepared for her Oscar winning performance.

"So, Mum is home, but when she read my note, she got muddled and thought I was staying the night here. She can't come and get me this late so asks if it's OK for me to stay with you. I can sleep on the sofa. I don't mind."

"Gee, of course it's fine!" Mrs Gray replied, relieved that the situation was getting resolved. "We've got a perfectly good spare room, so there's no need to sleep on the couch."

Begrudgingly, Jayne loaned Fiona a clean pair of pyjamas that gave off an aroma of fabric softener and showed her to a small room at the side of the bathroom. Although it was boxy, the single bed was inviting and the window looked out over the paddock where Beauty and Bella munched contentedly on the grass. It was perfect.

Once the door was closed, Fiona checked the bedside cabinet for any reading material, but found the drawer and the unit bare. She looked under the bed, but there was an empty void. She sat watching the dark shapes of the ponies for an hour before crawling between the clean sheets. It all felt weird and sterile, not like her creaky bunk bed at home with the crumpled sheets that smelled of… well, her.

The house was silent except for the distant roll of the waves against the cliffs to the back of the house. She lay awake, her mind still busy from the exhilaration of winning the quiz final in London, and pulling off the deception to stay the night at the Grays' house. She'd almost forgotten that it was her birthday. The treats of the day were more than she would normally receive. She hoped that she could extend her visit into the following day and be involved in whatever plans the family had. Maybe there was a gymkhana, or a trip to the cinema. She hadn't worked out how to negotiate that part of the plan, but would figure something out tomorrow.

Several hours later Fiona was still staring at the ceiling, unable to settle into sleep. Occasionally she heard a barking sound, but decided it was a fox rather than a dog. The ponies whinnied every now and again. With a frustrated sigh, she sat up in bed and pulled back the curtain to look out on the tranquillity of the paddock and the stable block beyond. On impulse, she pulled her trainers onto her bare feet and tugged her jacket over the top of her pyjamas. It was time for a night-time wander.

She had perfected the stealth of a cat burglar from her regular night time jaunts, and tip toed soundlessly along the landing. She paused at the top of the stairs and heard soft snores coming from behind the closed bedroom door of Jayne's parents. The Grays' stairs wouldn't creak. They were wooden and sturdy, built from quality materials, so Fiona crept down to the hallway without a sound.

There was a latch on the front door. This was too easy. She secured the mechanism that would allow her to get back in again, and skirted around the perimeter of the house to avoid detection.

Beauty raised her head as Fiona approached and, with encouragement, sauntered over the fence so that Fiona could ruffle her mane and pat her solid neck.

"You need a good brush," Fiona muttered to the pony, observing knots in the mane and streaks of mud down her hind quarters. "Let's go and see what we can find in the tack room."

Just like the store in the pub garden, the Grays didn't lock their outdoor buildings. The first door creaked as she opened it, but Fiona figured she was far enough from the house for the sound not to carry. The smell of hay hit her nostrils and she realised this was the feed store. There were plastic sacks of pellets lining one side of the room, with bales of straw and hay stacked neatly at the back. Fiona walked in and took a deep breath. The smell was comforting. She stuffed a handful of pellets in her pocket, before moving on to the brick building next door. This time, an aroma of leather and stale sweat hung in the area, with the saddles balancing on brackets on the wall, and bridles hanging alongside them. On the shelving on the back wall were buckets full of utensils. Fiona peered in and found what she was looking for. There were brushes, combs, hoof picks and other tools that she had no idea how to use.

She took a bucket and made her way back out to the paddock, tempting Beauty over to her with a palm of pellets outstretched to the mare.

With the gentle breeze rustling through the trees, and the waves pounding rhythmically on the rocks beyond the black perimeter, Fiona had a soothing soundtrack to work to. Beauty stood patiently as Fiona brushed through her mane, then changed to a softer brush to work her way across the horse's body. It was relaxing and therapeutic.

"That's a big improvement," Fiona told the horse, stepping back to admire her work. The coat was now free of dried mud, and even in the dim light of the moon, had a glossy shimmer. Fiona ran her hand over the horse's back and contemplated the prospect of putting on the saddle.

Beauty nudged her pocket, asking for reward for standing so obediently, and Fiona pushed the thought of tacking up to the back of her mind. Maybe next time. Once she'd spent more time with Jayne and been shown how to tack up properly, she could stay over again and come back for a midnight ride.

"Wait there," she told the horse, picking up the bucket and returning it to the tack room. Once stowed as she found it, she returned to the feed store to grab some final treats for Beauty.

It seemed darker than the first time she'd stepped inside and before her eyes could adjust to the dark, she caught her toe on something sticking out into the gloom.

"Bugger," she swore. It was a word that she'd heard both Daryll and her mother curse frequently. She bent down to rub her toe through the trainers and to get a closer look at the offending item that has assaulted her.

It was a metal chest, around knee high and resembling something that pirates keep treasure in. It was the coolest thing Fiona had ever seen. There was no lock on the hinge, so curiosity drove Fiona to lift open its heavy lid. Inside, clear plastic bags of sugar were stacked neatly to the brim of the chest.

Fiona knew that horses liked sugar, but usually in lumps and not bagged up like this. There was so much of it! She removed one bag from the pile and gave it a squeeze. It felt like the kilo bags of sugar that her mum bought. The ones that sat on the countertop in the kitchen and ended up full of crystalline blobs stuck together where Daryll kept putting a wet teaspoon in.

She was sure the horses wouldn't mind donating one of their many bags to the Farr family. It was payment for the neat hair treatment she'd just done, and her mum would be so chuffed with the present.

Fiona stuffed the bag in her jacket pocket, grabbed a handful of pellets that she gave to Beauty as she passed, and retreated back to the guest room with silent stealth.

26

"I can't believe how busy it is for eleven o'clock at night," Trudy said to Leon as they watched London at night through the windows of the black cab.

"I don't think anyone will still be up in Clover Bay," Leon agreed. They were making their way to the bookshop for the launch of the next instalment of the Zygon series, and both were tingling with anticipation.

Leon would have liked to have walked the two and a half miles from the restaurant, but he glimpsed Trudy's summer sandals and offered to pay for a taxi. The last thing he wanted was to get half way and have her moaning that her feet hurt. He'd had a good evening so far. The dinner was satisfying, the night air was warm and inviting, and a walk would have been the perfect way to round off the meal.

Throngs of people made their way around the streets, some heading back from theatres, meals, and bars, whilst others were heading onto nightclubs, night shifts or, like Trudy and Leon, to book signings.

"It's nice to visit London, but I couldn't live here," Trudy observed. "It's far too frenetic. I'm glad we didn't take the tube. Can you imagine how packed that would be at this time?"

Leon could imagine and was more than happy to cover the expense of a taxi to avoid it.

"Here we are," the cabbie announced, pulling up in Piccadilly. "Looks like you're not the only ones here!" He chuckled, and with dismay, Trudy saw a long line of fans queuing down the street for several blocks.

Leon thanked the cabbie and paid, before walking a hundred metres to find the end of the queue.

"I thought we'd be in plenty of time," Trudy lamented. The signing was still an hour away, and she'd hoped to be one of the first in the line.

"I'm sure they won't run out of books," Leon reassured her. "This bookstore knows what it's doing. It's been going for over two hundred years."

"You should have kept up with your writing," Trudy observed. "This could have been you signing books today."

"Nah," Leon shook his head. "I wasn't good enough." He thought back to the short-lived writers' circle at Jayne's house. "It's got to be effortless to be a good writer. The ideas, the characters, the plots, and the ability to paint pictures using the exact words. I just couldn't do it. I tried, but would overthink everything and then just tear it up thinking it was a load of rubbish. I figured I'd leave it to the experts like JJ Broome. Turns out I was more proficient at jointing meat," he laughed.

"Don't put yourself down. Not many people would use the word 'proficient' in a sentence. I don't think a lot of youngsters would even know what it means. That was the downside of scrapping cycling proficiency in schools."

They both fell silent for a moment, remembering how they pedalled around the playground, learning to signal at pretend junctions and stopping for invisible red lights.

"I'm enjoying this break," Leon admitted. "I was a bit sceptical, you know, about whether we'd have anything to talk about after 30 years, but it is fascinating seeing Fiona and Miss Earle again."

Trudy nodded in agreement.

"And you," he continued. "You were always bright, caring, and organised at school, and the years haven't changed that at all. Don't take this the wrong way, but you seem a bit adrift now that the kids have grown up."

"I still have Robbie at home," Trudy replied, wondering how Leon had so quickly tapped into the secret part of her that yearned for something meaningful to happen in her life. "He'll be off to secondary school in September, so he's quickly becoming an adult."

"I have a proposition for you." Leon was straight-faced. He'd been mulling over ideas for a few weeks, but talking to Trudy gave him clarity on his plans. "I have a decent sized space at the side of the shop that isn't being used for much. I've been wondering what I can do with it, and being here in the queue has given me an idea. It could be transformed into the most amazing events space. We could hold things like book signings, or do wreath making classes in the run up to Christmas, maybe cookery demonstrations..."

"Wine tasting," enthused Trudy. "Craft sessions, talks and meetings..."

"That's it! I knew you'd be full of ideas. I haven't got time to organise or oversee that myself, so wondered whether you'd like to be my events manager? Come and work for me."

"I'd love to," Trudy replied, "but I haven't got any experience in that sort of thing".

"Somehow I don't think that's going to be a problem," he smiled back. "I'm being dead serious. Come and see me at the shop next week and I'll convince you."

Leon's attention was broken, as there was shuffling in the queue ahead. He couldn't make out whether anything was happening but it was too early for the doors to have opened.

"Someone's coming down the queue announcing something," Trudy observed, leaning out to see along the line of bodies. Above the animated chatter of the waiting fans, it was impossible to make anything out.

A well-groomed girl finally bounced her way to their part of the queue.

"Hi everyone, thank you so much for coming tonight. We'll be opening the doors in just fifteen minutes." There was an excited cheer from a large Scouse family ahead. "Just to warn you, though, that JJ Broome will only be signing books and meeting people for an hour. After that time, we have pre-signed copies available to purchase but you might not get to meet the author in person…. being this far back in the queue, I'm afraid."

"That's rubbish!" exclaimed one of the Liverpudlians.

Leon's heart sank. He was hoping to ask him why he shied away from the public eye. There was so little information online about the writer, and he certainly didn't court fans through social media accounts the way that other notable authors did.

"We're so sorry, but authors need their beauty sleep too. Fingers crossed for you," she beamed, flicked her long ponytail and flounced further down the queue to repeat her spiel and disappoint more fans further back in the line.

Trudy was less bothered. She had promised Robbie a signed copy but hadn't specified that it would be personalised. She just hoped they wouldn't run out of the signed copies before they arrived at the door.

"I wish we'd found Jayne," Leon said suddenly. "I wonder what she's like now."

"I reckon she married well. Her husband is probably head of MI5 or a fancy lawyer, so she can be a stay-at-home housewife. She bakes cakes, goes to the hairdresser regularly and looks after her numerous brainy children."

"I reckon her kids would have weird names, like Clover, or Opal, or Atlas."

"Or Fortuna," Trudy giggled. "Can you imagine if we'd been told at school that Fiona would have a daughter called Fortuna!"

They shuffled up a further few metres but were still depressingly far from the entrance. They'd drawn level with the grand facade of Fortnum and Mason. Someone had toiled hard with summer-themed displays, where products had been temptingly mingled amongst pretend fields full of corn, poppies and sunflowers. Fake butterflies rose up the backs of the exhibits adding bright colour and a contrast to the drab concrete London Streets on the other side of the glass.

The minutes ticked by and they heard Big Ben announce the stroke of midnight. Trudy and Leon made out the faint countdown from the crowd up ahead as the doors opened. Trudy did some calculations in her head, figuring that if JJ Broome was able to sign and make small talk to one person a minute, he would only get through sixty people. She counted the heads ahead of her and could see sixty people in the space of a few Fortnum windows, meaning that there was no chance of meeting the author tonight.

Nevertheless, they waited patiently in line, creeping ever nearer the doors, but as Trudy feared, it was nearer to two o'clock by the time they reached the store.

The bookshop staff appeared weary and keen to close up and go home. They had the unenviable task of explaining again that JJ Broome had finished the meet and greet, and pointing disappointed fans in the direction of the stack of pre-signed copies. Trudy took two from the top of the palate, handed one to Leon and opened up her copy to the first page that announced it was an "Exclusively Signed First Edition". A scrawl underneath in black ink showed that JJ Broome had at least touched the page.

"Right," Trudy went into mum mode. "Let's pay for these and get back to the flat. We'll have to creep in so that we don't wake Fiona and Max."

27

The distinctive sound of Stock, Aiken and Waterman blasted out the speakers in the penthouse apartment thanks to the compilation CDs Fiona had thought to bring along. Fortuna insisted that there were new ways of listening to music these days, like streaming from the internet, but Fiona found it more reliable and comforting to be able to see the metal disc go into the machine and press the button marked with the play symbol.

After bidding farewell to Miss Earle, she and Maxine strolled back along the Thames, pleased that the evening had gone well. Conversation flowed, despite the decades that had passed since they last saw each other. The food was amazing and, better still, Leon had gallantly paid for them all.

"I should come to London more often," observed Maxine. "There's so much more life here than in my sleepy village." She observed the jubilant groups of friends that still sat around the restaurant tables. Ambient chatter filled the balmy riverside air.

"I live down a lane that doesn't even have streetlights," agreed Fiona. "There are some days when the only person I see is the postman."

Maxine could identify with that. With Grant in London during the week, days could go by without her speaking to anyone. The job at the spa was more about keeping her sane than bringing in an income.

"Not that I could cope with a nightclub anymore. Something biological happened when I turned thirty and I just want to drink wine on the sofa in my pyjamas now."

"Then that's exactly what we should do," Fiona decided. "There's more wine in the apartment, so we can have a good ole' girly chat in our nightwear."

The London skyline looked impressive from the penthouse through the inky darkness of night. Lights twinkled from buildings on the opposite side of the river, with red beacons shining out from numerous cranes dotted along the horizon. London was forever evolving. Fiona remembered visiting Canary Wharf with Alex twenty years earlier, and the same churn of construction was underway then. She opened the patio doors to let some breeze come through.

An hour later, the girls were slouched on the sofa cushions in their nightwear, the wine flowing and Rick Astley blasting from the speakers promising to never let them down.

"You know, it's occurred to me that you and me are quite similar," observed Fiona, topping up her wine glass. There was the slightest hint of a slur in her words as the alcohol took effect.

"We are?" Maxine was momentarily horrified.

"We are the brave ones," Fiona clarified. "The ones that didn't want to settle in Clover Bay for a boring life, but we grasped the opportunity to move away and make lives for ourselves."

Maxine recalled Fiona leaving because her mum dragged her to London, but let the discrepancy slip. She stole a glance at her friend but there wasn't a hint of irony in her features.

"We both like quality clothes," added Maxine, desperate to add something to Fiona's argument. She had noticed the good cut of Fiona's tea dress earlier and, although the matching shoes were on the frumpy side, they were from a designer that Maxine approved of.

"I do now," agreed Fiona, "but back in Clover Bay we didn't have any money. I had to wear Darryl's cast offs and the cheap shit that Mum bought in the market. Do you remember the naff weekly market in the car park near the lake?"

Maxine shook her head but the question appeared to have been rhetorical, as Fiona continued. "Even when I started work, I had to get all my skirts and blouses from charity shops."

"There's nothing wrong with that," Maxine replied. "I've picked up some really good vintage pieces in second-hand shops." She took a large glug of wine as another similarity struck her. "Oh, we both married into family businesses."

"Good one!" Fiona praised, raising her glass to Maxine. In her woozy state, wine sloshed over the edge, and Fiona rubbed the wet patch absentmindedly from where it landed on the cushion. She was glad Fortuna wasn't here to witness that. She had promised to keep the apartment in the pristine condition that they found it.

"And we're living comfortably off our husband's wealth," Maxine giggled. Fiona felt disloyal for not being offended, but it was true. Ever since the night of the dinner party where she and Ted made their relationship public, Fiona had officially become linked to Ted, and with that came his fortune. She'd carried on working for Foxhams initially, although negotiated a move to the London Bridge branch. She persuaded Ted to let her move so that she wouldn't have to travel on the tube with her growing bump, but in reality, it felt appropriate to be away from Alex. However, once Fortuna was born, she became a full-time mother and money was just there for her to access. Upon Ted's death, the paperwork dictated that everything was hers. The business, the house, the bank accounts, and the investments.

"I don't mind doing hard work if I need to," Fiona protested.

"Oh, me too," Maxine agreed. "I pitched in when Grant needed me, but the more successful he became, the less he needed me to input. Now that he's doing his deals in London, I have no idea what he's up to."

The two girls fell silent, the moody tones of Sade setting a sombre tone.

"I guess we're both abandoned by our men and cast adrift," Fiona offered. "I don't know about you, but most of the time I'm pretty bored and lonely."

She had a point, and there was no argument to be made. Maxine realised they probably did have quite a lot in common.

"Hey, you should come and visit me in Sevenoaks!"

Maxine smiled at Fiona. "I'd like that." She realised that she meant it. There was no reason not to rekindle a friendship after all this time. They both had free days and could fill the void in each other's lives.

"I'm surprised you never had kids," Fiona said, suppressing a drunken belch that was threatening to surface. She wouldn't have been so bold to raise the issue without all the wine that had flowed through her. Maxine groaned inwardly. She hated the topic coming up and thought that she was now safe from people questioning her life choices. When she and Grant first married there were the inevitable questions from friends and parents about when the patter of feet would be heard.

Maxine's answer was always the same. We'll see, we're still young, and there's plenty of time. Grant would just grimace in reply, and naively Maxine thought it was just an act. They never discussed it in any depth as Maxine presumed it was just a matter of time before "the right time" would present itself. She watched Grant kick footballs around with his nephews and admired how he spent hours sprawled on Trudy's living room floor with Ben and James building new developments out of Lego. He'd explain the importance of good square footage in office developments, and remind them not to forget a lift shaft for disabled access.

"He's so good with the kids," Trudy praised one weekend in the late 1990s as the sisters lazed on the sands of Clover Bay. They watched Grant in the shallows playing frisbee with the boys. The youngsters didn't tire of the game and Grant had been at it for hours, chasing after the plastic disc, splashing around in his swim shorts. He was athletic and competitive even at this, Maxine observed fondly. He'd make a great dad.

"Those kids adore you," Maxine told Grant as they made the three-hour drive back from Clover Bay to Leicestershire. Grant was at the wheel. He liked the control of driving, and Maxine couldn't bear the way he became a backseat driver whenever she drove. He winced if she hit the brakes too hard, or hesitated too long at a junction. Besides, his Audi was a monster compared to the Volkswagen Polo that she drove at the time. It was just easier to let him drive.

"It's nice to give them back at the end of the day, though, isn't it?" he replied, changing down a gear to overtake a Sunday driver.

"I can just imagine Trudy and Jason's evening," he continued. "It'll be getting the boys fed, bathed, sorting out their clothes for school tomorrow, then getting them to bed, and it'll be past nine o'clock when they finally sit down, knackered and thinking about having to get to bed themselves so they can do it all over again tomorrow. Us, we'll be enjoying a nice Cotes du Rhone at seven o'clock and enjoying some telly without interruption."

"Don't you ever imagine what our kids would be like?" Maxine asked. "I think if they had my looks and your brains, we'd have created perfection."

Grant frowned and gave a snort that sounded ominous. "Don't give it too much thought, darling, as it's never going to happen."

Maxine left a respectful pause. "Never say never," she persisted.

This time Grant looked at her for as long as it was safe to take his eyes from the road. It was the first time she realised he was deadly serious. His baby blue eyes that she fell in love with were suddenly ice cold.

"I am not having kids," he stated firmly. "I don't want children, I've never wanted children and I've always made that clear."

Maxine opened her mouth to reply but couldn't find any words.

"They completely take over your life. Dirty nappies, lack of sleep, tantrums, then drain your bank account for twenty years... I don't think I need to go on."

Maxine turned to look out the passenger window. She felt anger well up. This wasn't just about him, their marriage was a partnership, and why should he call the shots? Everything always seemed to be about him. It crossed her mind that she could easily "have an accident" with contraception, but the more she let the scenario run in her head, the more she realised how that could backfire.

She clung to the hope that he may change his mind, but he never did, and here she was in 2011 facing the question from Fiona that she most hated in life.

"We're just happy having Trudy's kids as nephews," she replied. "Kids of our own were just never on the agenda."

It seemed to satisfy Fiona, who topped up the wine glasses.

"So, tell me about Fortuna," Maxine said, swiftly deflecting the conversation away from her childless existence. "That's quite a name!"

"She's named after the Greek goddess of fortune," Fiona explained. "Fortuna was the personification of luck, so we chose that name because we were so lucky to conceive her." Fiona had told this lie so many times she almost believed it herself. She told Maxine how Ted was going to have his vasectomy reversed after their marriage, but miraculously she managed to conceive on the honeymoon. The one-in-a-thousand chance. It was the story they'd told family and friends. With British reserve, nobody challenged the inconsistency when Fortuna was born barely six months after the wedding.

Fiona stood up to go to the loo and realised that the lounge was beginning to spin.

"I think I'm going to head for bed," she said, steadying herself on the back of the sofa. She looked down to Maxine. Maybe one day she'd be good enough friends with Maxine to tell her the whole truth.

Yes, that would be nice.

28

The day of Ted's funeral was cold and crisp. It was a perfect November day with clear blue skies and a frost that turned the garden ghostly white.

He would have approved of the way he died. He'd just finished taking a swing at the ninth hole when the cardiac arrest struck. He'd felt flutters in his chest all morning, but wasn't going to pass up on his round with long-term friend, Nick. He'd been beaten last time and Ted's competitive spirit dictated that the pair replayed to give Ted the opportunity to break even.

He watched the ball sail in a perfect arc towards the distant flag when he simply crumpled to the ground before seeing that he'd hit a hole in one.

Nick was one of the best people to have around in an emergency. He was calm and rational, but there was little he could do in this scenario. The hole was one of the furthest from the clubhouse, and defibrillators were still a rarity in 2007. Realising the nature of the emergency, he'd called over to the nearest golfers and instructed them to call for an ambulance whilst Nick attempted CPR on an unconscious and unresponsive Ted.

The groundsman spotted the commotion from where he was pottering around on his buggy, and rushed over to help. Within minutes, golfers and staff converged. Many knew Ted, some by name, some just as a passing golfer. One of the regulars, Gerry, volunteered to sprint over to alert Fiona whilst Nick travelled in the ambulance with Ted. It was clear there was little point taking the patient to hospital but nobody wanted to verbalise it.

Ten days later many of the same crowd returned to the golf club for the wake. It was the only place to hold it that made sense. The captain closed the course for the day as a mark of respect and offered a greatly reduced rate on the catering. The salmon and cream cheese sandwiches looked delicious but Fiona could hardly bring herself to eat anything.

She had felt numb ever since Gerry had crashed through the kitchen door to break the news to her. Every day was a blur of people coming to help with arrangements, a conveyor belt of hugs, hands on her forearm, sympathetic faces and hushed conversations.

Ted's daughter Angela left Brighton and moved back into her childhood bedroom to help with arrangements and provide support. In reality, Fiona didn't see much of her. She spent long periods painting in her room, sleeping in late and going for lengthy walks, but Fiona was grateful for some company, especially in the dark evenings after Fortuna was put to bed and the house fell eerily silent.

At Ted's beloved golf club, the atmosphere had lifted for the wake. Guests were telling funny stories about things Ted had done in his younger days, and people laughed freely without feeling disrespectful to Ted's memory. A sense of relief spread through family and friends that the sombre proceedings were over, and the party for Ted was underway.

Fiona's head ached from the tension of the morning, and the pressure of being centre of attention at an event that wasn't hers to dominate. By mid-afternoon, she was hot and agitated. She knew she wasn't supposed to bail early, but there were no rules, and no-one could deny her this.

"Do you want to head home, or stay a bit longer?" she asked Fortuna, who was glumly skulking in the corner with a glass of Coke. She was approaching her sixteenth birthday, and had already blossomed into a confident, sassy teenager. She regarded her mother through thick black lashes and smiled wearily. "I'm OK. I owe Barney another game of pool."

"I'll walk back with you," Alex offered, overhearing. He had drunk more than he intended, putting away several large glasses of Ted's favourite Scotch whisky. The way that the liquid burned as it slid down his throat was consoling.

As they left the clubhouse, the November air was harsh and Fiona pulled her woollen coat tighter around her. She'd need to light a fire when she got home.

"Did Dad ever tell you about the time I broke into the clubhouse?" Alex asked. They strode along the public footpath through the golf course which provided a short cut to the lane.

"No," Fiona smiled for the first time that day. "What happened?"

"I was about thirteen, I guess, and staying over with a friend who lived just up the road in Seal. His name was Keith and he was really goofy. He'd never had alcohol before. I think his parents were really strict or something, but he wanted to try it. I'd had wine and stuff before, so it wasn't a great deal for me, but I really wanted him to try it. Like it didn't feel fair that he was being denied it. So, we hatched a plan to escape the house at midnight and go to the golf course and break in so that we could steal some booze from the bar." He paused, enjoying memory. "I don't think we waited to midnight. It was dark and we were excited, so we crept out the back door. Can you imagine it, two youngsters wondering through the night?"

Fiona remembered the times she went on midnight walkabouts at a much younger age and nodded. She wasn't about to confess her childhood wrongdoings, though.

"We got to the club and it was pitch black, but I hadn't worked out how we were going to get in. We tried all the doors and windows but of course they were locked shut. Keith was making these comments about how useless I was, and I was desperate to prove him wrong, so I decided to smash the glass. There was a fire exit door that was all glass so I found a massive stone down at the tree line and lobbed it. The whole bloody door shattered into millions of shards."

"Wasn't it alarmed?" Fiona asked. At an early age she had developed thought processes that questioned whether there would be CCTV, alarms and security guards in any given situation.

"Exactly!" Alex laughed. "The alarm started wailing and it sounded so loud. Bloody Keith got shit scared and ran home, waking his parents up to tell them what I'd done."

"I guess you never got invited to sleepover at his house again."

Alex shook his head.

"I was grounded for what felt like forever. I've never seen Dad so mad. Keith's dad came marching up to the house in the middle of the night to tell him what I'd done. Dad was mortified because it was his beloved club, and he had to go and tell the committee that it was me that had smashed the door. I had to write a letter of apology and Dad made an obscene donation to the club's funds to compensate."

Fiona nodded. "Money can make a lot of things right."

They walked on in silence, their steps in harmony on the gravelled path.

"I'm so going to miss him," Alex said suddenly. "His colourful cravats and positive attitude. His loud voice booming off the office walls as he got animated about the smallest of things."

Fiona glanced over and saw tears pooling in the corners of his eyes. "You and me both, Alex."

She wrapped an arm around his waist and drew him closer to her. She enjoyed the additional warmth emanating from his body.

"Poor Dad," Alex continued. Tears had escaped now and slithered down his cheek, but he let them fall. "He always had my back. Always. He paid the deposit on my first flat, he gave me a job that was beyond my capability and experience and carried me for many years because I didn't know what the fuck I was doing and wouldn't admit it." Alex sniffed hard and Fiona offered him a tissue.

"Then came the whole Alice episode." He paused while he blew his nose, and wiped his eyes on his coat sleeve. They'd reached Rose Cottage and automatically took the path around into the back garden.

"Let's sit under your mum's tree for a bit," Fiona suggested, pulling Alex over the lawn towards the bench under the cherry blossom tree. The branches were naked and unremarkable in their winter slumber but Fiona knew how this tree transformed into a glorious blaze of pink in the spring. She would bury Ted's ashes under the tree to reunite him with Diana. He'd probably have preferred to be in an urn at the golf club, but this was the one decision Fiona could make on his behalf.

They sat on the cold metal bench as Alex's last words registered. "What Alice episode?" Fiona asked.

"I probably shouldn't tell you," Alex agonised. He realised that the whisky had loosened his tongue, but the cold was sobering him back up.

"The Alice that worked in our Chelsea branch?" Fiona asked, thinking back sixteen years to her job in Foxhams. She couldn't think of any other women called Alice. With her pregnancy progressing, Fiona had transferred to the London Bridge branch, but she couldn't recall anyone ever mentioning Alice again. "Whatever happened to her?"

"Oh God," Alex cringed, realising that he was going to have to elaborate. "She was let go. Kind of."

"Why? What did she do?" Fiona normally enjoyed a drop of scandal, but felt this one may not be what she wanted to hear. "Ted never mentioned it."

"The poor girl didn't do anything," Alex replied, shaking his head in shame. "I tried to touch her, you know, a bit inappropriately, and let's say that she was more resistant than you."

"And you sacked her!" Fiona was too appalled at his confession to be embarrassed about the way she acquiesced to his advances every time.

"No, no, she kneed me in the groin, which I totally deserved. I was such an idiot."

"You were," Fiona agreed. "You were bloody married at the time as well."

Alex bent forward and buried his head in his hands. His shoulders shook momentarily and Fiona couldn't tell if he was crying or laughing.

"That doesn't answer the question of why she was let go," Fiona prompted. The sun had dropped below the horizon now and the air was bitter now. She shivered.

"A bit of time went by, and I stupidly tried it again. I wondered whether she was one of these girls that was playing hard to get. Turns out she wasn't. This time she went to Dad and complained of sexual harassment." Alex paused. Fiona had never seen him look so defeated. "Dad cleared up my mess yet again. He organised a payoff that would buy her silence and compensate for the inconvenience of having to leave her job. But in the process, it all came out. All the dirty laundry everywhere. She'd guessed about me and you, and told Dad. She told him that she'd found the condoms in my desk drawer and stabbed all the packets with a drawing pin without me knowing." Alex was crying again.

Fiona groaned. She'd protested so hard to Ted that she hadn't slept with anyone else, whilst all this was going on in the background. The more she had betrayed Ted, the kinder he had been to her.

"So, Ted must have put two and two together about Fortuna," Fiona mumbled, hating herself for what she'd done. "He took our mess and cleared it up."

Alex wiped his eyes again and took Fiona's hand. "He did. But no-one else knew, and never will. Let's never breathe a word about this again." He looked Fiona in the eyes and realised how quickly he had sobered up. "I'll always have your back. Anything you need, just let me know."

As if on cue, Fortuna strode into the garden, her heels wobbling on the gravel. Barney and Katrina were in tow, ready to call it a day and head back home. Barney was now nineteen and able to drive his parents home.

"What are you doing sat there?" She called to them. "It's freezing."

Fiona stood and pulled Alex up off the bench behind her. "You're right," she replied. "Let's go and get the fire going inside."

29

The last Sunday in June was bright and sunny, just as it had been thirty years earlier. Perfect conditions for recreating the photo. There was no professional photographer this time, so Maxine had nominated herself to take the picture. Grant had a decent digital camera that he loaned her for the task, making sure to give her a few lessons in depth of field and framing the subjects first. She had the original photo with her so she could place everyone in the position they were in originally. Except Jayne of course.

"Hey, you look brilliant!" Maxine praised her sister as Trudy emerged from the bedroom in a navy pleated skirt and sky-blue blouse. It was an adult replica uniform of the 1981 quiz team. Clover Bay junior school hadn't had an official uniform but for the quiz final Miss Earle insisted they should dress in smart matching outfits for the occasion. Trudy had scraped her shoulder-length hair into two side bunches, just as she wore in the original photo. Only now she had boobs and wrinkles.

"Sasha found me some navy shorts in Cotton Traders," Leon joined the party, managing to replicate his 1981 self with knee-length shorts. The buttons on his shirt strained against his pot belly. With his bushy beard and hefty frame, he was the least like his 1981 image.

Fiona was last to emerge into the kitchen.

"Ow, my fucking head's banging," she grumbled. "He much did we drink?" She glanced around the stack of empty wine and champagne bottles and didn't need a response. The glasses had already been washed and put away by Maxine who had risen early and taken advantage of the gym facilities. They were basic, but she combined it with a sunny run along the Thames and felt great.

"I don't want to rush you but we said we'd meet Miss Earle at ten o'clock," she fussed.

Trudy had the trophy, and Maxine remembered to stuff Hector in the camera bag. Together the trio from the quiz team, plus a glamorous Maxine headed back out onto the Thames path to make their way to Westminster Bridge.

They weren't late, but Miss Earle had once again arrived before them

140

and was waiting in the exact same spot that provided the backdrop thirty years earlier. In 1981 she had worn a navy skirt and jacket to match the students and it was pleasing to see that she had once again made the effort. Her husband of twenty-five years tagged along out of curiosity. As coach to the Westminster School quiz team, he was enthralled that the winning team had found each other again, and were proposing to recreate the image. Following the meal, Susie had filled him in on how the brain boxes of Clover Bay were now working in a supermarket, running a farm shop and volunteering in an animal sanctuary. Hardly the titans of industry or business tycoons she had imagined they might be.

With the introductions and pleasantries out of the way, Maxine took the camera out of the bag and started to assemble the team according to the original picture.

"So, Trudy this end," she bossed, "with Fiona next to you, and put your arm around her shoulder." The ladies got into position and Maxine realised that being five feet tall instead of three feet was going to have implications for where Big Ben would be framed. "Then Leon next to you." She paused, realising that Jayne would have been next. "Miss Earle was crouched next to you in 1981, but that's going to look a bit silly."

"It's probably better if I crouch," compromised Leon, "and you stand behind me, or lean on my shoulder." They tried out the position and Maxine looked at the scene through the viewfinder. Tourists were starting to push past the group on the bridge now, herds of all nationalities, pointing excitedly at the clock tower and snapping pictures of the river and the Houses of Parliament beyond.

"Who's going to hold the trophy?" asked Trudy.

"It's probably appropriate for me to have it?" A voice came from behind Maxine, and she whirled around to see whom the accented tones belonged to. The group all looked the lady up and down. Her eyes were obscured behind oversized sunglasses, but everything else was neat. Her blonde hair was cropped short and in place as though she'd just stepped from a hairdressing salon. Her complexion was flawless with lips coloured fascia to match her silk dress and heels.

"Jayne?" Leon was the first to find his voice, and the blush followed suit. Jayne removed her glasses and casually slipped them into a large tote hanging from her shoulder.

"My God," gasped Trudy. "We tried to find you but it's like you vanished."

"I live in Canada," Jayne replied by explanation. "I still follow Clover Bay news on Facebook and saw this was happening and I was curious. Happily, it coincided with a work engagement, so here I am." There was a beat where everyone wondered how to greet their long-lost friend. Should they shake hands, or pull her in for a bear hug? There was something in

Jayne's manner that suggested she wasn't in the mood for either.

She stepped in between Fiona and Leon and reached out to take the trophy from Trudy, who was still agape with disbelief.

"I'm on a tight schedule though, guys, I have a flight home from Heathrow this afternoon."

"You've got time for a drink with us afterwards, though, right?" Maxine asked. "There's a lot of catching up to do."

"I don't think I do, no," Jayne replied with no hint of apology. "Let's do this photo." She proffered the trophy towards the camera with her perfect smile. The gang were stunned into obedience and all took their places. Maxine tossed Hector to Trudy to hold. The lucky mascot had to share the occasion. With the camera held to her face, she took several snaps, shuffling around to get various angles. It would never be as perfect as the original but that wasn't the point.

"There. Done." Maxine confirmed. "Give me your email address then I can send you a copy, and we can all keep in touch." She pulled a small notebook from her handbag and found a pen buried in its depths. Jayne wrote her email address down whilst Maxine packed the camera away.

"So where did you go when you left Clover Bay?" Leon asked. "You left so suddenly… without saying anything." He was trying not to sound accusatory.

"Canada," Jayne replied simply. "My mum and I went back to Canada whilst my sister and Dad got taken to some safe house whilst they assisted the police with their enquiries." All eyes remained on Jayne for further explanation, which she seemed reluctant to give. She checked her watch with a flicker of irritation. She lowered her voice so that it was difficult to hear what she was saying. "Nina had got herself involved with a drug dealer. Her boyfriend was smuggling drugs in, bringing them up the cliffs at the back of our house and storing them in the tack room." She looked directly at Fiona. "But you knew that, right?"

She handed the trophy back to Trudy and placed the shades back over her eyes.

"Got to dash. I mustn't miss that flight. Bye now." With the briefest of waves, she began to walk away leaving the gang staring after her in disbelief.

"Did that just happen?" Maxine asked the others.

Fiona's brow was furrowed. She didn't understand why Jayne directed the last comment at her. Why would she know anything about drug dealers or…?

"Fuck me!" She mumbled to herself. Suddenly the penny dropped. The memory came flooding back of her ten-year-old self gleefully presenting her mother with the bag of sugar as a present from the Grays. The bag she had stolen from the tack room on her midnight walkabout. She had been upset when her mum's face clouded over and she demanded to know where she had got the sugar from. A brief argument ensued when Fiona's mum refused to believe that Mrs Gray would give this bag to the family as a present. In the end, Fiona stomped up to her room, thinking what an ungrateful bitch her mother was. Of course, it wasn't sugar, it was a fat bag of contraband cocaine. She could only imagine that her mum took it straight to the police and caused the chain of events that led to the family's abrupt disappearance.

"It was nice of her to find the time to stop by," Miss Earle said with a wry smile. "And if we recreate this photo again in twenty years at least we have an email address for her."

Maxine glanced down at the piece of paper where Jayne's neat handwriting graced the page.

"Well, a postal address at least," Maxine confirmed. "She's said that she'd like her necklace back with a copy of the print." Maxine blushed, and her hand shot up to the glass pendant that adorned her neckline. "And to send it for her attention - JJ Broome - courtesy of her UK publishers, and put the address…"

"JJ Broome!" squealed Trudy, inspecting the piece of paper over her sister's shoulder. "Are you telling me that Jayne is JJ Broome?"

The gang all stared after Jayne who was now just a brief flash of fuchsia merging into the crowds at the southern end of Westminster Bridge. Once again, she vanished from their lives.

OTHER BOOKS BY C. FLEMING

Dark Horse

Londoner Abigail Daycock is a fashion graduate drifting through her twenties in a stream of temping roles whilst waiting for her life to get going. After making an innocent computer error that brings down the banking system, Abigail is forced to go on the run from the police with nothing but a tent and a handful of cash to survive on.

Hiding out in the sleepy Gloucestershire hamlet of Sloth, Abigail meets a cast of colourful characters that shake her from her comfort zone and change her destiny forever.

Staying on Track

Staying on Track is the sequel to Dark Horse.

Abigail's contentment shatters as soon as her Christmas present trots into her life. The feisty ex-racehorse, Moody Muppet, seems intent on pushing her
patience to the limit.

The horse's arrival coincides with a mountain of challenges for Abigail. Struggling with money worries and loneliness, she is further frustrated by the interference of Molly, Sam's right-hand woman. As Abigail reaches breaking point, she faces the biggest decision of her life. Will the gift horse prove to be the final straw, or the saviour, of Sam and Abigail's future?

Drowning

For 18-year-old Poppy Winter, life on the self-sufficient island of Socius is bliss. She spends her simple days tending crops, sharing out the produce and enjoying secret fantasies about Stuart.

On the neighbouring island of UMAH, President Monterey's daughter Fenella is juggling a hectic mix of cello recitals, a law degree and her fated infatuation with the son of her dad's political rival.

The two girls have the opportunity of a lifetime when they embark on a cultural exchange to sample each other's life. But it's not long before they are both out of their depth.

Printed in Great Britain
by Amazon

33391923R00086